A DARING DECEPTION

BY
AMANDA BROWNING

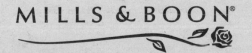

MILLS & BOON®

MILLS & BOON and MILLS & BOON with the Rose Device are registered trademarks of the publisher.

*First published in Great Britain 2000
Harlequin Mills & Boon Limited,
Eton House, 18-24 Paradise Road, Richmond, Surrey TW9 1SR*

© Amanda Browning 2000

ISBN 0 263 82010 6

*Set in Times Roman 10½ on 12¼ pt.
01-0008-45997*

*Printed and bound in Spain
by Litografía Rosés, S.A., Barcelona*

'Did it ever occur to you, Nathan, that I'm not the person you think I am?'

Nathan's lips curved mockingly. 'No, but you couldn't seriously expect me to. I'm one of the few people who know from experience that there's more to you than meets the eye.'

Rachel laughed out of sheer disbelief. 'You truly believe that you know me that well?'

'Like I say, I've seen both sides of you. One I can respect, the other... Well, we both know what you're capable of.'

She shook her head helplessly. 'You're wrong, you know. There is no other me.'

His brows rose sceptically. 'Are you asking me to believe that you're a reformed character? Sorry, darling, but as the saying goes, a leopard cannot change her spots.'

'You're very sure of yourself, aren't you?' she asked through gritted teeth.

'Very sure. Remember that if you're ever tempted to take me on.'

Oh, she was tempted all right, and when the time was right, she would act.

Amanda Browning still lives in the Essex house where she was born. The third of four children—her sister being her twin—she enjoyed the rough and tumble of life with two brothers as much as she did reading books. Writing came naturally as an outlet for a fertile imagination. The love of books led her to a career in libraries, and being single allowed her to take the leap into writing for a living. Success is still something of a wonder, but allows her to indulge in hobbies as varied as embroidery and bird-watching.

CHAPTER ONE

Rachel Shaw gritted her teeth together in silent annoyance and paced back along the corridor. It was hot today, and the silk of her white blouse and black skirt clung uncomfortably to her skin, emphasising her hourglass figure. Her long legs, encased in sheer nylon, carried her back to the other end in seconds. As she eyed the lift, and the mute testimony of its closed door, her strikingly beautiful face, with its large green eyes and generous mouth, lost its customary serenity and took on a sternness that only one man could produce. Nathan Wade. This was typical of him. Absolutely typical. The only time the damned man was punctual was for a date with some beautiful woman or other.

Immediately she winced, knowing that was unfair. Nathan was good at his job, managing the merchant bank her great-great-grandfather had set up in the last century, and he took it extremely seriously. It was simply that when it came to answering a summons from her grandfather he could be counted upon to turn up only when *he* was ready and not a moment before. It was her own ridiculous jealousy talking.

What a joke that was. She, who, after her parent's disastrous marriage and messy divorce, had declared she would never fall in love, and had never dated

any man for more than a few weeks, had fallen like
a ton of bricks for a man with the same attitude, and
was now green with jealousy. She hated the thought
of him with those other women, but there was nothing she could do about it. Not even if she knew how.
Because, for reasons she had yet to fathom, Nathan
Wade had taken an instant dislike to her. Nothing
in the past two years had changed that.

She refused to allow it to worry her, even though
his attitude had at first angered, then hurt her. An
emotion she most certainly did not like. She had her
fair share of pride, and refused to let him catch even
a glimpse of her true feelings. Which was easy when
they rarely came into contact with each other. By
day she ran a catering business with her cousin,
ranging from private parties to small functions. They
were both cordon bleu trained, and because no job
was too small business was booming. By night,
when she wasn't working, she had an extremely full
social life, being seen at all the in places, though
never with the same escort for long. That aspect of
her lifestyle hadn't changed.

Recently, though, she had had to juggle two jobs.
Her grandfather Linus Shaw's private personal assistant had had a serious accident and was recover-
ing slowly. By rights he should have brought in a
temporary assistant, but, being Linus, he hated
change. Therefore he had turned to Rachel, his favourite granddaughter, for help. She, as he had
known full well, had been unable to refuse him, so
for the past few months she had been helping him
with his not inconsiderable correspondence, and aid-

ing him in the writing of his memoirs. He had been, she was discovering, every bit as flamboyant as Nathan Wade, which was probably why they fought so often. Notwithstanding that, there was genuine respect and affection between the two men, and they would probably get along much better if Linus was less fond of issuing orders that Nathan generally ignored.

As a rule, Rachel could sympathise with the younger man, but there was something about this latest summons which was different from the others Linus was worried, and that was why she was pacing the floor outside the spacious flat overlooking Kensington Gardens that Linus Shaw had called home since his retirement from the world of high finance.

She took yet another glance at her wristwatch, and even as she did so the lift doors slid silently open, revealing the single male occupant. Her head came up and her heart did its customary flip-flop at the sight of him, although it hadn't taken her long to learn what a waste of time it was to be attracted to this particular man. He had the attention span of a goldfish when it came to women, and changed them as often as he changed his socks. That was the irony of it. Of all the men she could have fallen for, she had had to pick one with an aversion to commitment just as she had.

In those circumstances it shouldn't have bothered her that he didn't like her, but it did. She didn't know what she had done to offend him. Ordinarily she would have taken the bull by the horns and demanded to know the reason for his disdain, only her newly sensitive heart had quailed. Did she really want to know? Would it change anything? The answer to both questions having been no, she had kept her feelings well and truly hidden behind a disdainful contempt of her own for what she termed his alley-cat proclivities.

However, that didn't stop her being pleased to see him, though she would rather eat worms than let him know it. Which was why right now her forehead creased into a frown of disapproval.

'You're late,' she informed the man who had pushed himself away from the wall and stepped out into the expensively carpeted hallway.

Nathan Wade's right eyebrow lifted quizzically. 'Miss me, sweetheart? I didn't know you cared.'

Rachel snorted, wondering for the trillionth time why he alone had to have a voice which crept along her spine like the softest of soft caresses. Instinctively she stiffened her backbone an extra notch. 'I don't. For myself. If you never turned up again I wouldn't lose a wink of sleep.' Great Rachel another lie to add to an already long list! To think of never seeing him again made her feel strangely queasy inside. 'However, my grandfather seems to think highly of you. Why escapes me, but these things happen. I put up with you for his sake.'

'As a dutiful granddaughter should. Especially as you are far and away Linus's favourite, and therefore must loom large in his will. Something you wouldn't want to put at risk,' Nathan remarked sardonically, making her blood boil. Her love for her grandfather was very real, and had nothing at all to do with money.

'Don't be so disgusting!' she protested sharply, and found herself under the unflinching scrutiny of a pair of fine blue eyes.

'He still thinks butter wouldn't melt in your mouth, doesn't he? What does he think of the array of chinless wonders that wander in and out of your life?' Nathan probed, and Rachel's eyes narrowed wrathfully.

'You're a fine one to talk, Nathan Holier than-Thou Wade! How many boxes of long-stemmed red roses did you send out to women this time?' she asked, saccharine-sweet in lieu of answering his question.

Nathan had been touring the European branches of the world-renowned bank for the past several weeks. She doubted very much if he had remained celibate the whole time. In fact, if he had had the use of a company jet, she was pretty sure he would have taken along some light female entertainment to relieve the boredom!

Rather than taking offence, Nathan let his lips curl into a damned attractive smile. 'One or two. I forget the exact number.'

She sent him a withering look, even as her heart twinged. 'I bet you do.'

'You know, that sounds an awful lot like sour grapes to me, sweetheart,' he drawled, getting under her skin with the skill of a surgeon.

Despite her best efforts, the little green-eyed monster was alive and well inside her. Notwithstanding,

Rachel afforded him an old-fashioned look. 'Credit me with some intelligence. I'd have to be mad to want to get involved with a man like you. Fortunately for me, insanity doesn't run in my family,' she responded dryly.

'There are a lot of women out there who don't see it as insanity,' Nathan argued, with a reminiscent gleam in his eye.

'The operative words being "a lot of women",' Rachel returned smoothly. 'Florists all over the world must rub their hands together with glee every time you pull into town.'

He laughed, a deep-throated sound which almost set her knees wobbling. Damn, but the man had everything. He was tall, dark and handsome, with a body to die for, and a dimple in his cheek when he smiled that was downright sinful. It was an unjust world that had such men in it. Rachel groaned silently.

'I do my bit for the economy.' Nathan grinned roguishly, showing her, had she needed proof, why it was women fell for him in droves.

'More than your fair share, I would think,' she retorted waspishly, unable to help herself, and had him laughing again. 'I'm so glad I amuse you,' she added tartly.

'It's either laugh at you or kiss you, sweetheart,' he countered, bringing colour to her cheeks once more.

This was a new tack, and her nerves jangled. 'Don't imagine for even one second that I would let you kiss me!' Rachel declared in outrage, only to see a faint smile curve his lips.

'Darling, if I wanted to kiss you, then kissed you would be.'

Her throat closed over. Why all this talk of kissing? What game was he playing in that devious mind? Whatever it was, she wanted nothing of it. She drew herself up to her not inconsiderable height of five feet eleven in her two-inch heels, and folded her arms with a belligerent lift of her chin. 'Not whilst I had a breath left in my body!'

Nathan's eyes gleamed. 'Now that sounds suspiciously like a challenge. Are you daring me to kiss you, Rachel?' he charged softly, and the sound of her name on his lips, instead of the more usual 'sweetheart' or 'darling', did strange things to her breathing.

Did she want him to kiss her? Only all the time! She dreamt of it constantly, wondering how he would feel, how he would taste. But she wasn't about to find out just to amuse him. She sent a warning flashing from the depth of her emerald eyes. 'Lay so much as a finger on me, Nathan Wade, and I'll break your arm.'

Blue eyes gleamed as he considered the threat. 'Could you?'

Rachel allowed her lips to curve faintly. 'Do you think I couldn't?' In this day and age a wise woman learned how to defend herself, and Rachel had taken several self-defence courses. She had yet to put anything she had learned to the test, but she knew a few moves which she was sure would surprise him.

Nathan appeared to think so too, for he shook his head ruefully. 'Something tells me I would be a fool to call your bluff, and my mother didn't raise her children to be fools.'

Realising the threat, whether real or imagined, had passed, Rachel relaxed her stance. 'It's a pity she didn't do more about other areas of your character.'

'She knows I'll settle down when the right woman comes along,' Nathan countered smoothly, understanding her perfectly, and she arched a dubious brow at him.

'And just what will make one woman the right one?' she asked curiously, interested in spite of herself.

He shrugged. 'I haven't the foggiest idea, but I'll know her when I see her.'

Which clearly left her out of the running, even if she hadn't been already. 'In the meantime you'll just carry on in the same old way, loving them and leaving them?' Rachel remarked dryly, to which he grinned unrepentantly.

'Until somebody invents some other way, it looks like I'm stuck with it. Now, delightful though it always is to share these interludes with you, sweetheart, perhaps you'd care to tell me what your grandfather's summons is about this time.'

Rachel's cheeks pinkened uncomfortably as she was brought back to the point of Nathan Wade's presence, and at how far they had wandered from it. It was another thing she so much disliked about loving him, this infernal habit he had of making her thoughts stray from the path they should be taking. She had intended keeping everything cool and to the point, but history had repeated itself…again.

Collecting her thoughts, recalling her own lingering sense of unease, she frowned faintly. 'I'm afraid I can't,' she said unhappily.

'Has the old codger sworn you to secrecy again?' he charged with some amusement. 'OK, I won't compromise your principles by asking you to tell me, but you can at least give me some sort of hint,' Nathan urged in a tone of voice that Rachel knew would, on most occasions, get him his own way. This time, however, he was going to be disappointed.

Had she not already been uneasy about the reasons for this summons she might have made some flippant response, but instead she looked at him seriously. 'I can't because I haven't the faintest idea why Linus wants to see you. All I do know is that something is bothering him in a way I've never seen before, and he won't let me help. I don't mind admitting I'm worried, Nathan, really worried.'

'Is he ill?' he asked sharply, clearly concerned, which raised him in her estimation, but Rachel shook her head.

'Grandfather had a medical check-up only two weeks ago, and he was fine.' She quickly allayed any fears he had in that direction. 'No, this is something entirely unexpected. Something apparently only you can help him with.' She looked at him with a directness that had Nathan taking a deep breath and dragging a hand through his hair.

'If it was any other man I'd suspect woman trouble, but not Linus. OK, you'd better take me to him. The sooner I find out what's going on the happier I will be.'

Rachel led the way to the large room her grandfather used as a study. Linus Shaw glanced up from his seat at one half of an enormous old partner's desk. He was a handsome man in his late seventies, still in fairly robust health and sporting a full head of pure white hair. He drew the ladies every bit as much as Nathan did, though his heart would always belong to the adored wife he had lost eight years ago.

Far from looking pleased to see his much liked successor, a grunt of disapproval left his pursed lips. 'Took you long enough to get here!' he growled.

Nathan ignored the less than friendly greeting, and strolled over to the desk. 'Unlike you, I haven't retired,' he countered. 'I came as soon as I could.'

'You took as long as you thought you could get away with!' Linus harrumphed knowingly, and Nathan grinned unrepentantly.

'I was born with a dislike of being ordered about. I take after you in that respect, Linus,' he replied teasingly, but the older man did not look one whit abashed.

'The trouble with you, my lad, is that you've no respect for your elders.'

'On the contrary, I have nothing but respect for you, sir. What was it you wanted to see me about this time?' He made the question sound long-suffering, but Rachel knew better. He wasn't taking this at all lightly.

Having remained just inside the door until that moment, she now took a step forward. 'I'll go and check on those points we were discussing yesterday, Grandfather, and leave you two to talk in private. Shall I bring you some coffee before I go?'

'Don't run off, Rachel. I want you to sit in on this.'

This request was so out of the ordinary that Rachel exchanged a startled look with Nathan. 'But surely if this is a private matter, then...' Silently she sought his guidance.

Nathan didn't look best pleased, but his response was to give the merest hint of a shrug which suggested they humour the older man. At least for the moment. 'You'd better make a pot and bring three cups, Rachel. We'll wait for you.'

The kitchen was a high-tech dream, with every modern appliance, and was generally ruled over by a very efficient housekeeper. However, Mrs O'Malley was away for a few days, and, though Linus was quite capable of looking after himself, Rachel was quite happy to make the odd cup of tea or coffee in her absence. It took her very little time to brew the coffee, place the pot and three cups on a tray and carry it back to the study.

In the interim Nathan had pulled another chair up beside the desk, but he rose when she came in and took the tray from her, setting it down on the desk. Taking her own seat, she dispensed the coffee, and it was only when they were all seated again that

Linus Shaw took a deep breath and revealed what was on his mind.

'I need your help on a matter of the greatest delicacy, my boy.'

'You know I'll help in any way I can,' Nathan responded, and received a rather wry smile for his pains.

'You may want to take that back when you hear what I have to say, but I'm going to hold you to it, just the same.'

Nathan grinned. 'You always do, sir,' he returned, sitting back in his chair and making himself comfortable. 'Fire away.'

However, having been given the encouragement he required, it was a long moment before Linus finally nodded to himself and began to speak again. 'What I am about to reveal to you is a secret that has been kept for the better part of fifty years. It concerns an old and dear friend of mine.'

'I take it this old and dear friend is a woman,' Nathan remarked dryly.

'A lady,' Linus corrected firmly. 'In every sense of the word. And before you ask, Rachel, she was never more than a friend, to both myself and your grandmother. Of course there was a man involved— I cannot tell you his name; suffice it to say he was a noble personage of a somewhat obscure European enclave. They would most certainly have married, had that been humanly possible. Sadly, it was not.' The regret in his voice was very real, and, recognising the implications, Rachel asked the obvious question.

'What stopped them? Were they both married already?'

'He was; she was not,' Linus amended. 'Being who he was, divorce was out of the question. The marriage had been a necessary joining of two powerful families. It was not a love match. Though I do believe there was mutual respect, and genuine love for their children, there was no grand passion. My friend and—we'll call him the Archduke—met by the merest of chances, and fell deeply and irrevocably in love. They were, however, sensible people. Neither given to reckless or ill-judged actions. They had a choice to end the matter there, before getting in too deep, or continuing the romance as discreetly as possible.'

Rachel was utterly fascinated by this unexpected tale of romantic intrigue. 'What did they decide?'

'They chose to end it, of course. Too many people could have been hurt. Neither was happy, but they stood by their decision. Their lives drifted on, as lives tend to do, until one day, a long time later, their paths crossed again. It seemed to both of them that fate had taken a hand. Unable to walk away a second time, they began an affair.'

'How long did it last?' Nathan queried.

'For more than thirty years,' revealed, surprising both his listeners. 'Of course the couple were discreet. They had a difficult life, picking up moments here and there, treasuring them, because they did not know when the next would come. Only death could part them, and that was how it turned out to be. The Archduke died not so very long ago.'

Nathan gave a soft whistle. 'And nobody knew?'

The old gentleman's face took on a grim expression. 'Just a few good friends—or so we all thought. But it seems not to be so.'

'Somebody spilled the beans,' Nathan remarked gravely.

'In a manner of speaking,' Linus confirmed. 'There were letters.'

'Love letters?' Rachel checked, with a wince, and he nodded.

'They were written over that thirty-year period, and always kept safely locked away from prying eyes. Unfortunately during a recent party at my friend's house the letters were removed from their hiding place.'

'What did the police say?' Rachel asked, naturally, and Nathan quirked an eyebrow at her.

'She wouldn't have told the police. Police make reports. Reporters ask questions. The next thing you know, the whole story is on the front of the tabloids and on prime time TV.'

'Exactly,' Linus agreed. 'After nearly forty years of discretion, the very last thing she wanted was for the whole of her private life to come out. Not to mention how distressing it would be for the man's family. No, there could be no police, which was why she wrote to me.'

'She wants you to get the letters back?' Nathan asked in no little amazement.

'But how?' Rachel frowned.

'The method is up to my discretion,' the old man replied, and her lips parted on an 'o' of surprise.

'Are you saying she knows who took them?'

'The thief was a man called Luther Ames,' Linus revealed, with such a wealth of distaste in his voice that it was obvious to Rachel he had some prior knowledge of the man.

She had never heard of him. 'Who is Luther Ames?'

It was Nathan who answered. 'A playboy. A man with no visible means of income yet who always has plenty of money to throw around. His main hobbies appear to be collecting expensive antiques and gambling.'

'He also happens to be my friend's nephew. He attended the birthday party at her home on the day of their disappearance. The letters were kept in a drawer of the *bonheur du jour* in her bedroom. Unfortunately she had been called away upon some errand earlier in the day and had forgotten to lock it. Forgetfulness is one of the curses of old age. During the evening she discovered Ames coming out of her room. Oh, he made some believable excuse for being there, but later she found the letters were gone.'

'But the affair ended years ago. What point is there in taking these letters now?' Rachel argued.

'Because although the affair is over the man's family are still very much alive,' Nathan responded grimly, receiving a nod of confirmation from her grandfather. 'The threat of the disgrace is as strong as it ever was. I take it Ames wants money for the letters' return?'

Linus sighed heavily. 'No. When my friend demanded he return the letters, he said he would—provided she did him a little favour.'

'You mean he's prepared to blackmail his own aunt? That's despicable!' Rachel exclaimed angrily. The man had to be a monster.

'It certainly explains how he manages to always have money to spare, despite his lifestyle. He's probably done this before,' Nathan observed bluntly. 'What are his terms?'

Linus grimaced. 'He wants her to use her influence with a certain company to make sure a take-over goes ahead. A take-over which will increase his personal fortune by several million pounds. Naturally, she flatly refused. However, time is running out, and, the situation being what it is, she cannot dare him to publish and be damned. She has to get the letters back, for she knows that if she does not he *will* use them. For all his charm, he has a vengeful streak if he doesn't get his own way. She knows it, and so do I. The only sure way of knowing the matter is closed is to take the letters back—fast.'

At that, Nathan went quite still. 'And you need my advice as to how to go about it?' he charged, in a strangely toneless voice which had Rachel glancing at him sharply.

Linus looked him squarely in the eyes. 'No. I need you to steal the letters for me.'

For a moment Nathan simply stared at him in stunned silence. 'You cannot be serious.'

Immediately Linus raised a calming hand. 'Oh, not *steal*, exactly. Retrieve would be a better word.'

Nathan uttered a bark of laughter. 'Steal or retrieve; there's very little difference between the two. Whichever way you put it, it's breaking the law.'

Linus's gaze narrowed. 'I never expected you to be so nice,' he said sharply.

'Nice? I think I'm entitled to be a little alarmed when you ask me to break into Ames's house and do some thievery of my own,' Nathan protested reasonably.

Linus tutted irritably. 'Don't be a fool, boy. I don't expect you to break in at dead of night. I expect you to be *invited* in,' he declared. 'Once inside, you'll have every opportunity of searching the house.'

'You have it all figured out, don't you?' Nathan observed in mingled amusement and incredulity.

'I don't like to leave things to chance,' Linus concurred.

'Then perhaps you can tell me how I am to get invited into Ames's house? Just walk up to the front door and ask if it's OK if I stay for the weekend? Oh, and by the way, whilst I'm here do you mind if I search the place for some letters you stole?' Nathan said facetiously, causing Linus to glower at him.

'You don't have to do anything. All you will need is Jasmine to run interference.'

Both Rachel and Nathan blinked. 'Who?' they chanted in unison.

'You know,' Linus snapped tetchily. 'That blonde woman you're going out with. What's her name...? Jasmine, or something equally ridiculous.'

Rachel hastily stifled a giggle and received a

quelling look for her pains. 'Her name is Jade, and for your information we are no longer an item,' Nathan replied tightly.

'Then take someone else. Who *are* you dating at the moment?' Linus ordered.

'At the moment I'm not dating anyone,' Nathan said through gritted teeth.

'What do you mean, you're *not* dating? You always have a woman around somewhere! Can't keep your hands off them!' Linus exclaimed irritably.

Much to Rachel's amusement, faint colour stole up Nathan's neck. 'Well, I'm sorry, but I don't have one. I had no idea it would be required.'

Linus's fingers tapped out a staccato sound of annoyance on the desktop. 'Then you'd better go out and get one! Damned quickly too!'

A muscle ticked in Nathan's jaw, and Rachel watched it in fascination. 'Does she have to be blonde, or will any colour do?'

'Of course she has to be blonde. Ames has a thing for blondes. He likes them decorating up his house, apparently. Curse your fickle heart, Nathan. You're putting the whole plan in jeopardy. There are three real passions in Ames life: blondes, antiques and gambling, and you and your girlfriend were to supply two of them. A double entrée into his house. But you need to catch his eye. I understand Ames is going to be in his American home at Lake Tahoe this weekend, and I had everything planned for then. He's bound to keep the letters close to him, and who knows when we'll get another opportunity like this?

You'd better go out and pick up the first blonde you meet.'

The outrageous suggestion appeared to echo round the room, and Rachel thought Nathan was in imminent danger of exploding, he was so furious. However, with a monumental effort of will, he forced himself to relax. 'For your information, I do not pick up women off the streets.'

The two men stared each other out for what seemed like ages, then Linus grunted. 'You don't, eh?'

Nathan crossed his arms and shook his head emphatically. 'No.'

Linus sank back in his seat with a heavy sigh. 'Then Lord knows what's to be done.' he declared morosely, upon which Nathan closed his eyes for a second.

Rachel leaned over and placed her hand over her grandfather's. 'We'll think of something, Grandfather,' she murmured consolingly, and felt rather than saw Nathan's head turn towards her.

'I must be mad to suggest it, but this whole situation has a ring of insanity about it. If you can spare her, I'll take Rachel.'

Rachel very nearly fell off her chair in shock. She gasped, fish-like, for a moment before a word passed her lips. 'What?' she squawked incredulously. He couldn't have said what she thought he had.

Linus was as surprised as she, and his response was to look her over critically. 'Of course I can spare her, but...Rachel hardly fits the bill,' he con-

cluded doubtfully, bringing colour to her cheeks and
a flash of fire to her eyes.

'What does that mean, exactly?' she demanded in
outrage, her feminine pride tweaked by the implied
criticism.

The old man's expression was regretful. 'Forgive
me, Rachel, but I only have to look at you to see
the problem. You're blonde, certainly, but far too
intelligent. I'm glad to say not Ames's type at all,'
he replied gently, and she did a rapid mental review
of herself.

She could see what he meant. She wore suits because they were comfortable to work in. Her long
blonde hair she kept tied back in a knot at the nape
of her neck because she hated it falling over her face
whilst she worked. Last, but not least, she wore
glasses for all the close work she did on the com-
puter. All in all, Rachel was not the blowsy blonde
type that Luther Ames apparently went for in a big
way. Which was just as well, really, because he
didn't sound like a man she would want to get to
know.

'I agree she doesn't look the type now, but she
could be made to be,' Nathan put in quietly, sending
a shock wave through her system. What on earth did
he mean by that?

Linus frowned. 'I admit the potential is there, and
Rachel is a quick study, but she's no actress,
Nathan.'

Nathan was watching Rachel, a calculating look
in his eye. 'Oh, I don't believe it would take long
to make her convincing.'

'You think not?'

'Trust me. It can be done with very little time or effort.' Nathan declared confidently, bringing her eyes to his face.

There was a certain something in his expression which made her frown and go still. She tried to read his thoughts, but it was as if a wall had gone up. Confused, and vaguely unsettled, she finally found her voice. 'Just a second. Will you please stop talking about me as if I weren't here? Time is irrelevant. I have no intention of going anywhere.'

'But I'm counting on you, Rachel!' Linus exclaimed in disappointment. 'There's no time to find somebody else.'

Whilst she hated the thought of letting her grandfather down, this was way beyond her agreement to help him in his time of need. 'I'm sorry, Grandfather, but I simply can't do what you're asking. Even if I could just drop everything and fly to America, leaving my business to sink or swim which I can't—you were quite right. What you need is a *femme fatale*, and that just isn't me.' Not that she didn't know how to be, but that was another story.

'On the contrary,' Nathan cut in softly. 'With a little make-up and the right clothes I can see you holding your own with the best of them in the playgrounds of the rich. Places like Tahoe or...Cap d'Antibes, for instance.'

The pause was infinitesimal, but it registered on Rachel, who blinked in yet more confusion. Why had he mentioned Cap d'Antibes in that strange tone of voice? And just what was that jibe about the play-grounds of the rich? What on earth was he suggesting? Yes, she had been there, but only once, and the circumstances had been extraordinary. She looked at him sharply, but before she could demand an explanation, Linus spoke.

'Thank goodness that's one problem solved. You'll take Rachel with you. If the whole mess can be sorted just as easily, we'll be laughing. Now, I've booked two seats on the midday flight to Tahoe to-morrow, and a suite at the Tahoe Caesar Hotel. The rest will be up to you.'

Rachel could feel control of the situation slipping out of her hands. 'Just a minute,' she protested. 'I haven't agreed to go.'

'Of course you'll go, my dear. Nathan needs you.'

If he thought that would persuade her, he was mistaken. She stood up quickly, the better to enforce her stance. 'I'm sorry, but it's quite out of the question.'

Nathan rose too, reaching out to take her arm in a deceptively firm grip. 'Don't worry, Linus, it's just stage fright. She'll go,' he declared unilaterally, and looked down at her with a clear message in his eyes for her not to argue. 'Let's talk it over, shall we?' he suggested mildly, but she knew it for the order it was, and bridled.

Yet, however fuming she might be, she was un-willing to cause a scene in front of her grandfather, and set her jaw firmly. 'Very well,' she agreed frostily, determined to stick to her guns. 'We'll talk, but I'm telling you now, you're wasting your time.'

'That remains to be seen, sweetheart,' Nathan murmured softly as he gently but firmly ushered her from the room.

CHAPTER TWO

NATHAN strode down the passage to the lounge, with scant care that she virtually had to jog to keep up with him, and urged her inside. The second the door closed behind them Rachel jerked herself free from his hold and turned on him.

'Let me make myself quite clear. We have nothing to talk about. I'm not going with you, and you'll have to explain that to my grandfather,' she insisted, half turning back to the door. Nathan promptly stepped into her path, preventing her intended departure. 'Get out of my way,' she ordered curtly, but he shook his head.

'I wouldn't be so hasty if I were you, sweetheart. Sit down. We might as well be comfortable whilst we talk,' he suggested, following his own advice by taking a seat on the couch.

Rachel stood her ground. She wasn't going to sit as she had no intention of staying. 'How many times do I have to tell you there's nothing to talk about? I have a business to run, and I can't just walk away from it at the drop of a hat. There's nothing you can say that will make me change my mind.'

'Not even Cap d'Antibes?' he challenged sardonically, and the way in which he said it had her breath catching in her throat even as she stared at him blankly.

'You mentioned the resort before,' she said, confused, spreading her hands to underline her incomprehension. 'I don't—'

'Don't what…? Remember?' Nathan supplied before she could finish, steepling his fingers and watching her over the top of them. 'Strange, I thought you had an excellent memory. It's one of the reasons your grandfather thinks so highly of you.'

Totally confused now, because he sounded so certain, Rachel placed a steadying hand on the back of the nearest chair. She had no idea what was going on here, but the undercurrent swirling about her made her want to shiver in purely primitive reaction.

'I was going to say I don't understand,' she ground out pointedly. 'All I know is you're talking in riddles and I simply don't follow you. Why don't you just say whatever it is you intend to?' she advised without preamble, but for all the notice he took of it, she might have saved herself the effort. Nathan wasn't about to be rushed.

'I can see how you might want to forget. Allow me to refresh your memory of the long hot summer you spent in the South of France three years ago.'

Surprise must have been writ large on her face as a glimmer of light appeared. It *was* three years ago that she had been in Antibes, but it hadn't been for the whole summer, and neither had it been a holiday. Far from it. The real surprise was what he appeared to be suggesting.

'You were there?' She sought confirmation. He nodded solemnly. 'I never saw you.'

That made him laugh, and it was a far from pleasant sound. 'Let's face it, sweetheart, you only had eyes for one man. The rest of us were invisible, including his fiancée. As an interested onlooker, I admired the way you went after him with such single-minded determination. Your inventiveness knew no bounds. What a performance. You wanted him and you made sure you got him, no matter what. Then, in the blink of an eye, you were gone. Nobody could figure out what had happened. As a matter of interest, what did make you leave in such a hurry?'

Her eyes widened as the realisation of precisely what he had seen came home to her. Her acting *tour de force* that summer had had a purpose beyond the obvious, but seen from the outside there was only one perspective anyone would have seen. Suddenly his attitude towards her became abundantly clear. He thought she was a… There wasn't a nice way of describing what he thought her. Of all the nerve! Not to mention hypocrisy. There were shades here of the pot calling the kettle black. OK, so he didn't know her side of things, and to give him his due it was easy to jump to the obvious and nasty conclusion. But he hadn't had to cling to it all this time! Clearly he didn't give anyone the benefit of the doubt.

A cauldron of intense rage began to simmer inside her. She should put him straight right now, but the memory of all the things he had said to her, all the insinuations, kept her lips tight shut. She was damned if she would. She would tell him only when she was good and ready.

The truth was she had gone to Antibes that summer with the express purpose of saving her cousin Emma from an ill-advised relationship. Word had reached the family that the man Emma had become engaged to whilst staying with a friend in the South of France was a fortune-hunter. The Shaw family, and its various branches, were extremely wealthy, and Rachel and Emma had sizeable trust funds in their names, though both had chosen to work for their living. With their business still at the fledgling stage, Rachel had decided to stay at home, so it had been the first holiday they hadn't spent together in years.

Which was how Emma had come to fall foul of Anton, because Rachel hadn't been there to advise her. Of course, when her parents had tried to intervene, Emma hadn't believed them, hence the family had turned to Rachel, who had gone in fighting as usual. She had flown over with the express purpose of making Emma see reason. An unenviable task, yet she had gone because she loved her cousin dearly and hadn't wanted to see her hurt.

Naturally, knowing Rachel's negative attitude towards love having lived through her parents' roller-coaster marriage and messy divorce, Emma hadn't believed her either. No amount of talking—and they had talked long into the night—had put a chink in Emma's rose-coloured glasses. In the end Rachel had been forced to take strong measures. If Emma was so certain that Anton was for real, then she, Rachel, wouldn't possibly be able to steal him away. Emma, just as stubborn as Rachel, had dared her to

do her worst. So she had, and that was what Nathan
Wade had seen.

Playing a man-eater had been relatively easy, for
Rachel had always had a natural aptitude for acting.
Basing her character on a girl she had known in
college, Rachel had thrown herself into the part of
a wild and wilful seductress who used her beauty
and her fortune to get whatever man she wanted.
She had pursued Emma's fiancé, and, being without
scruple, he had dropped Emma like a stone.

To cut a long story short, after several days of
watching her fiancé dance attendance on her cousin
there had been a showdown between Emma and
Anton. It had been an unpleasant scene, especially
when Rachel had revealed exactly who she was.
Anton had vanished after saying some very nasty
things, and once Emma had had a cleansing bout of
tears the two cousins had packed up and flown
home. The rest, as they say, was history. What neither of them had known, so wrapped up had they
been in their personal drama, was that Nathan Wade
had witnessed the juicier moments and taken his cue
from that.

Emma and Rachel still ran a growing catering
business, and shared a flat in London. That brief
interlude in France was long forgotten—except by
Nathan. Had he been a different man, Rachel
wouldn't have hesitated to clear the matter up forth-
with, but she was too incensed.

Instead of doing the sensible thing and making a
case for herself, she merely shrugged in her most
offhand way. 'How does urgent family business

sound?' she quipped lightly, and knew from the narrowing of his eyes it hadn't gone down well. Not that she cared in that instant. His opinion could hardly get any worse when it was at rock bottom already.

'Anton and his fiancée departed about the same time, too,' Nathan went on. 'I suppose they also had "urgent family business"?'

Rachel couldn't speak for Anton, but Emma certainly hadn't been able to get back to her family quickly enough. 'I imagine so. They didn't say,' she agreed blithely.

'Anyway, having seen you in action, you can imagine my consternation when I took over the running of the bank and found you were Linus's granddaughter.'

Rachel sank down onto the arm of the chair. She had no difficulty imagining that at all. Having caught her act and believed the worst, she understood why he had disliked her on sight. But why had he remained silent all this time?

'Why didn't you say something before?'

'I admit my first instinct was to confront you, but then I became intrigued. You looked so different from what I remembered. You acted differently, too. I began to wonder what you were up to. I waited to see what sort of game you were playing,' Nathan explained smoothly.

Her brows lifted in an arc of surprise. 'I wasn't playing a game,' she pointed out, and he half smiled.

'On the contrary; you play it all the time. You have that look of innocence down pat. No wonder

Linus thinks the sun rises and sets in you. Does he know anything at all about the men in your life?'

Her eyes narrowed at that. 'He knows I date,' she conceded cautiously.

Nathan laughed. 'That's a quaint way of putting it, but it keeps him happy, and that's the way you want it. The game you play, sweetheart, is to keep him believing you're still made out of sugar and spice and all things nice, when in reality your private life wouldn't bear scrutiny.'

She frowned darkly, thinking she understood him all too clearly, but seeking clarity before she hit the roof. 'My...private life?' she probed in a tight voice.

'You know, the things you get up to after hours. I don't care what man you've set your sights on now, or how you go about getting him. It's none of my business. What I do need, however, is for you to use that talent on Luther Ames. Use it to keep him occupied whilst I search for the letters.'

She was stunned by what he was suggesting. Now she understood his continued disdain. He had never seen her differently. All this time he had believed there were two Rachels. The one he saw during the day, who did her job and caused her family no harm, and the one who came out at night to prey vampirically on unsuspecting males. Dear God. It was almost too incredible for words.

Unable to sit still in the face of this, Rachel sprung to her feet, striding over to the window, battling to keep her temper in check. All this time, whilst she had been mooning like a lovesick idiot, he had believed her to be spending her nights having

a good time with countless men whose names she
doubtless couldn't remember! Ooh! Never mind that
she had, in fact, been a model of rectitude. In his
mind she was branded a man-eater, and so she remained to this very day. The injustice of his blindness made her see red, but she fought with her own
personal devil. She had promised her family she
would do her best to curb her instinct to respond
blindly in anger, but never had she needed to use
more self-restraint. Turning back to face him, she
folded her arms to hide the way her hands were
balled into angry fists.

'That's quite an opinion you have of me. Tell me,
Nathan, did it never occur to you that you could be
wrong about me? Did you ever give thought to the
possibility that I'm not the person you think I am?'
she asked in a seriously controlled voice.

Nathan's lips curved mockingly. 'No, but you
couldn't seriously expect me to. I'm one of the few
people who know from experience that there's more
to you than meets the eye.'

She laughed out of sheer disbelief. 'You truly believe you know me that well?'

'Like I say, I've seen both sides of you. One I
can respect; the other... Well, we both know what
you're capable of. We both know you can do what
Linus is asking of you. Why bother to waste time
denying your alter ego?'

She shook her head helplessly. Every word he
said was pushing her towards an outcome her family
knew only too well. When the devil got in her, there
was no stopping her, but she was prepared to give

it one more try. 'You're wrong, you know. There is no other me.'

His brows rose sceptically. 'Are you asking me to believe that you're a reformed character? Sorry, darling, but as felines go, you're as sleek as they come. A prime example. And, as the saying goes, a leopard cannot change her spots.'

'*I* don't need to change,' she argued through gritted teeth. 'Think about it. There hasn't been one breath of scandal linked to my name in all the time you've known me, has there?'

'I'll agree you're certainly more discreet than you used to be. I haven't heard any recent gossip about you,' he conceded dryly, and it was the way he said it which put her back up and had her teetering disastrously on the brink.

'Even with that you won't accept that you heard nothing because there was nothing to hear. Damn it, why do you find it impossible to accept that you're wrong about me? That there might be an innocent explanation for what you *think* you saw in Antibes?'

His expression became remote. 'Because I've known women like you before. I've seen all the tricks they use to blind a man to their true character, but what they all forget is that in the end nature will out. They always give themselves away.'

The scales began to tip dangerously. What he didn't say was that he considered her to have given herself away already. His arrogance was beyond belief. 'How can you make such a sweeping statement? Nothing is so cut and dried. Surely it's possible for at least *one* to have a change of heart?'

'Am I supposed to believe that's what happened to you? You saw the error of your ways and re-invented yourself?' he challenged incredulously, and she wanted to shake him till his teeth rattled.

She wasn't saying that at all, as he would know if he really knew her as well as he thought he did. Well, he was about to learn a great deal more. She went over the edge, waving caution goodbye. As far as she could see, she was damned if she did and damned if she didn't, so to hell with it. 'Oh, believe what you like! You will, anyway,' she snapped, with a defiant lift of her chin.

Nathan stared at her through eyes dancing with amusement. 'Maybe I'm wrong. Maybe you're now as pure as the driven snow. But frankly, sweetheart, that doesn't interest me right now. What does is that you know what to do and how to do it to get the best result,' he added trenchantly.

His patent disbelief fanned the flames of her anger. 'Perhaps I do, but that doesn't mean I'm prepared to help you.'

'You think not?' he murmured softly. 'Don't be too sure. Everybody has their price, Rachel. What's yours, I wonder?'

Rachel laughed hollowly. 'Don't try to blackmail me, Nathan. It won't work,' she pointed out as coolly as she was able.

'What if I were to put it this way? What would you do for my continued silence?'

The soft words seemed to ring around the room, and Rachel froze. 'I beg your pardon?' she asked in total disbelief.

He smiled mockingly. 'I thought that would get
your attention. I'll give you my ultimatum. Do what
Linus wants, and he'll never hear about your private
life from me.'

Rachel stared at him, wondering if she had somehow crossed a time warp into another life. He
couldn't be serious. How could he have rubbed
shoulders with her for so long and not know that
there was nothing to tell? Linus knew all about
Emma, had been the one to send her out to sort the
matter three years ago. He knew, too, about her inability to trust men after the way her father had be-
haved to her mother. He didn't know she had fallen
for this blinkered man he admired so much, though.

God, Nathan was so certain he knew her. So certain he was right. He deserved to have some of that
arrogance knocked out of him, and, the way she felt
now, she was just the person to do it.

Her heart began to race as she dealt with the
temptation. What pleasure it would give her to throw
the truth in his face! Her eyes narrowed in a way
that should have sent a wise man running for cover.
Nathan unwisely stayed right where he was. 'You'd
say nothing, ever?' she checked, and his eyes glittered with amusement.

'You're getting more like yourself by the minute,'
he observed mockingly. 'Do what Linus asks of you
and my lips will remain sealed. You can get any
man you want, any way you want, and yet you'll
remain as innocent as the day is long in Linus's
eyes.'

With a mental grinding of her teeth, Rachel rose

to her feet once more. 'Well, now, that does make a difference,' she mused thoughtfully, crossing to the mirror and making a show of smoothing her hair back. Tucking in a stray lock, her eyes darted to his reflection and caught the curl of his lip. It hurt to finally realise what his opinion of her was, but she was a fighter, not a quitter. He would get the person he thought her to be, in spades. Starting now.

'After all, I have nothing but Grandfather's best interests at heart,' she reasoned, and Nathan's smile broadened.

'Of course you do. Which is why you couldn't stand by and refuse to help him now, could you?' he enlarged simply.

Rachel smiled too as she swung round. 'It isn't that I didn't want to help him,' she explained with a shrug, getting into character.

Nathan appeared only too happy to follow her lead, which did nothing for her mood. 'Of course not. It's just that a girl needs to know where she stands.'

The rat. Her smile widened. 'Absolutely.'

'OK, now that we understand each other so much better, why don't you come and sit down and we'll make some plans,' he drawled sardonically, making her palms itch. He would never understand her. Never.

She didn't want to sit, but standing made her look tense when she needed to appear at ease. She chose the chair opposite. 'What sort of plans are you referring to?' she asked, determined to sound businesslike at the very least.

'Getting our stories straight, for one thing. We're supposed to be lovers. I'm the high roller and you're my lucky mascot. Think you can play the part?' he asked her with a decided glint in his eye.

Rachel shot him an equally mocking look. 'So long as you don't expect me to bring you luck.' What she wished for him right now was quite the opposite.

As she was fast coming to expect, Nathan laughed. 'Just remember we're on the same side, lover.'

Lover. The word shivered across her skin like the faintest breath of hot desert air. She didn't feel in the least lover-like. Murderous, yes. The trouble was, loathe him as she might for his blindness, she was still strongly attracted to him. The last thing she needed was for him to discover the fact, but how to prevent it when the pretence of their relationship would entail certain behaviour which would put her in close proximity with the man? Danger signals flashed. It would be as well for her to set the parameters of this fictional relationship right now.

'I'll remember we're on the same side, and you remember that we aren't lovers,' she told him bluntly.

He looked over at her with a faint curl of his lip. 'A fact for which I am extremely grateful. Rest assured I don't want you, and never will. Try any of your games on me and you'll regret it.'

He couldn't have said anything more guaranteed to get her dander up. She forgot in that moment that she didn't want him to want her and acted purely on feminine instinct.

'Oh, really?' she murmured with sweet viciousness. 'I've heard it said that people who protest too much generally have something to hide.'

He had no trouble following her drift. 'Some men might, but I'm not one of them. Now that we've got that out of the way, let's concentrate on the real problem,' Nathan responded evenly, and it annoyed her no end that she couldn't rattle him. She wanted to knock the wind clean out of him, and upset his complacency once and for all. She'd do it, too. Somehow. Before this was over. It was a promise she made to herself right there and then. She would find his weakness and use it against him. Everyone had their Achilles' heel—even men like Nathan Wade.

She eyed his bent head as he opened the envelope Linus had given him. 'You're very sure of yourself, aren't you?'

He looked up, blue eyes glittering sardonically. 'Very sure. Remember that, if you're ever tempted to take me on.'

Oh, she was tempted all right, and when the time was right she would act. 'I'll be sure and make a memo in my diary,' she drawled, and his teeth flashed whitely as he smiled in acknowledgement.

'So you don't know anything about Luther Ames?'

She shook her head. 'I only know what Linus said, that he prefers blondes.'

'Exactly. Just remember, although he prefers them, he's no gentleman.'

His warning surprised her, given his opinion. 'Don't tell me you're concerned about me, Nathan?' she charged with patent disbelief.

He sent her a reproving look. 'Don't take it personally. I'd worry about anyone who got tangled up in Ames's sticky web of corruption. A man who would stoop to blackmailing his own aunt doesn't have an ethical bone in his body. We don't know what else he gets up to. Keep your wits about you, but don't let him see you have any. His women aren't required to think, just look decorative. Add all their vital statistics together, and they still wouldn't reach your IQ. You should fit right in.'

Rachel came as close as she ever had been to smacking another human being. 'Are you trying to be deliberately offensive?'

He eyed her quizzically. 'Don't get your nose out of joint. I meant you'd fit in because of your talent for being all things to all men. You should be able to play a dumb blonde with your eyes shut.'

'Thanks, that makes it even worse!' she returned dryly. 'Do me a favour and don't pay me any more compliments like those.' *All things to all men!* He made her sound as if she spent her life on her back. Lord, but he was hateful. If it was the last thing she ever did, she would show him just how wrong he was about Rachel Shaw!

She became aware that Nathan was looking her over with a jaundiced eye. 'You're going to have to

ditch the glasses,' he declared flatly, and she nodded, for that was the least of her problems.

'I only wear glasses when I'm working, anyway.'

'I suppose you think they promote a different type
of image, like the suits,' he observed dryly, and
Rachel took umbrage.

'I take my work very seriously and I do my best
to appear professional at all times. There's nothing
wrong in that,' she pointed out acidly.

Nathan's expression spoke volumes. 'Rachel, are
you under the impression that by playing down your
looks you've lost the ability to turn men's heads?
Take it from me, it ain't so,' he informed her mock
ingly, and every nerve in her body jumped. 'When
it comes to sex appeal, sweetheart, you'd be oozing
it if your hair looked like a bird's nest and you wore
nothing but a sack tied up with a piece of string.
You might not flaunt it by day, but it's still there.
You're a sexy woman, and no amount of glasses and
power suits is going to change that.'

Considering she was not the person he believed
her to be, his description of her as sexy, indeed,
oozing sex appeal, came as quite a surprise. It meant
he had noticed her after all—not that that did her
the least bit of good when the woman he thought he
saw wasn't the woman he was looking at. The
knowledge hurt, and she responded accordingly.

'I'm more than just a body and a pretty face!'

'Maybe, but right now those are the only two of
your plentiful attributes we're interested in. They're
certainly all Luther Ames will see. Speaking of
which, the more he sees, the quicker he'll take the

bait, so remember to pack your sexiest clothes,' Nathan ordered.

Rachel knew that if she possessed any blatantly sexy clothes it was by accident, not design. She tended to wear more trendily casual clothes, not the designer dresses and evening wear he clearly expected. She would have to do some hasty shopping, though it would go very much against the grain. She didn't much care for the idea of dressing solely to invite men to ogle her, and was beginning to see where her anger had taken her. However, she was committed, and never let it be said that Rachel Shaw ran away from anything!

'I should be able to find something suitable,' she confirmed.

'We can always go shopping in Tahoe,' Nathan offered, and her nerves jolted.

'No!' she refused quickly. 'That won't be necessary.' The last thing she wanted was for him to buy her clothes. That would be going altogether too far.

Nathan shot her a mocking look. 'I'd pay. You don't have to worry about any of the bills,' he said dryly, and the embers of her wrath flared up again.

Her smile was a gem of fake sincerity. 'Oh, I wasn't, but, since you're offering, I'll supply the clothes, you provide the diamonds.'

As she had hoped, his amusement died instantly. 'Diamonds?'

This time her smile was entirely natural as she realised he didn't like the implication. 'You're a wealthy man, and if I'm your lover you surely must have given me jewellery. I always think a woman looks naked without diamonds. Oh, but you don't have to worry, I promise to give them back afterwards. I wouldn't want to appear greedy.'

Blue eyes narrowed to icy chips. 'Very generous of you. Is there anything else I should provide?'

Enjoying his irritation, Rachel's shrug was casual. 'I'll let you know if I think of anything.'

A muscle ticked at the corner of his tantalising mouth. 'I'm sure you will,' he said frostily, and she had to bite her lip to keep from laughing. Perhaps this whole situation would have its amusing side after all.

'Nothing cheap, mind. I have expensive tastes.' A calm smile tilted her lips as the lie was uttered. 'Oh, and I really don't care for rubies.'

A steely glint flickered in his eyes. 'No rubies. You have no objection to emeralds or sapphires?'

'None at all,' she retorted brightly.

'I'm glad to hear it. Now, if that's the end of the shopping list, we'd better get on,' Nathan urged, turning his attention back to Linus's list of travel plans and thereby missing her grin of delight at having soured his mood. 'Our flight leaves at midday tomorrow. I'll swing by your place about ten to pick you up.'

The suggestion had instant alarm shooting through her. She couldn't have him turning up at the apartment. If he saw Emma he was bound to recognise her, and that would never do. She wanted her pound of flesh before she hit him with the truth.

'That won't be necessary,' she refused politely. 'My…cousin will drive me,' she explained, hoping her hesitation would make him assume her 'cousin' was male, and no relative at all. It worked like a charm and had his lip curling cynically.

'OK, we'll meet at the airport. Just make sure your "cousin" lets you get some sleep tonight,' Nathan responded. Tucking the envelope into his jacket pocket, he took a quick glance at his wrist-watch. 'I have to leave. This business will make a mess of my calendar, and I'll have some important meetings to rearrange. Heaven alone knows how long this is going to take.'

'Surely a weekend should be long enough?' Rachel put forward hopefully. She had no wish to prolong the affair either.

Nathan smiled wryly. 'If I were Ames, I wouldn't leave those letters anywhere they could be found too easily. We may have to search the whole damned house. You'd better just hope and pray he doesn't have some state-of-the-art security system, or we'll be screwed before we start. We could both end up in jail yet,' he declared by way of a parting shot, and Rachel was left staring at the empty doorway.

She knew he wasn't joking. Getting caught in the act was a distinct possibility, and it was a sobering thought. They were going to have to be very, very careful. Yet no matter the possibility of dire conse-quences, the thought of backing out never entered her head. She was going to see this through to the end for the sheer pleasure of throwing the truth back in Nathan Wade's face.

CHAPTER THREE

SEVERAL hours later Rachel turned the key in the lock of her flat and stepped inside. Her cousin came through from the kitchen as she used her back to close the door again. Emma was as tall as Rachel, but dark where she was fair. Judging by her damp hair, she was not long out of the shower. There was a puzzled look on her face which turned to curiosity when she saw the large number of packages Rachel was carrying.

'What are you doing here? It's barely the middle of the afternoon. Is something wrong?' she asked as she came forward to relieve her cousin of some of the bags. When Rachel was helping her grandfather, she generally stayed till well into the evening.

'You could say that,' Rachel confirmed with a grimace, tossing her handbag and the other parcels onto the nearest chair with a stifled groan. Reaching up, she deftly removed the pins from her hair. It fell in a swathe of liquid gold about her shoulders, and she combed her fingers through it with a sigh of relief. 'Mmm, that's better. Been jogging?' Shrugging out of her jacket, she tossed it onto the chair too.

'Twice round the park, as usual,' Emma confirmed, setting the bags she held down with the others and curling herself up in a corner of the couch.

'How did the lunch go?' Rachel queried, referring to the catering job they'd had booked for that day, and which Emma had had to manage alone.

'Fine,' Emma confirmed. 'In fact, they were so pleased they've booked us for another two lunches, so things are looking up.'

'That's great. If we can get a good foothold in the lunchtime market that would be ideal.'

'My thoughts exactly,' Emma agreed, with a broad smile. 'Well?' she asked pointedly, watching Rachel take the other corner and kick off her shoes, wriggling her toes in pleasure. 'What's with this sudden desire to go shopping in the middle of the afternoon?'

By now the transformation was complete. No longer was she the Rachel Shaw who part-owned and ran a catering company. She stretched sinuously, showing off a figure few guessed lay hidden behind her professional clothes. Her glasses had already been consigned to their case on the journey home. This was the woman nobody got to see during working hours. The woman Nathan Wade had decided was a danger to all men.

'Would you believe I ran out of clothes?' she quipped, knowing that what she had to say would create a localised earthquake and wanting to put the moment off as long as possible. She had had time to calm down and calculate Emma's reaction. The prospects were grim.

'No,' Emma returned, as expected, and Rachel sighed, accepting the inevitable.

'OK, the truth is I had to go shopping because

I'm flying out to America tomorrow—to Lake Tahoe, to be specific—and I needed some new clothes,' she acknowledged, feeling her way carefully into a full confession.

'America?' Emma ejaculated in surprise, as well she might. 'Whatever for?'

'Because Grandfather asked me to,' Rachel expanded cautiously.

Emma immediately relaxed a little. 'Oh, it's work, then. What is it this time? Some research he needs done?'

'Not exactly,' Rachel amended wryly. 'You haven't asked me who I'm going with.'

Emma's perfectly arched brows rose. 'I assumed with your grandfather, but obviously I was wrong. Who, then?'

Rachel took a deep breath and plunged in. 'Nathan Wade,' she revealed, and held her breath.

'What?' her cousin exploded, sitting up like a jack-in-the-box. 'Have you gone out of your mind?'

'Very possibly,' Rachel returned dryly, sitting up too, and folding her arms around her knees, resting her chin on top of them. 'You don't know the rest of it.'

'There's more? Oh, Lord, Rachel, what have you done now?' Emma charged uneasily, well aware of her cousin's propensity for rushing in where angels feared to tread.

Her reaction had Rachel laughing. 'I'm glad to see you've not lost the habit of expecting the worst of me!' she teased.

'I know you too well.'

'Then you'll know I'm not going away with him for a week of sin.'

Emma groaned. 'I'd almost rather hear that you were.'

'You won't when you hear what I have to say,' Rachel countered with a grimace. 'Nathan thinks I eat men for breakfast. Not to mention lunch and supper!' she added ironically, but her cousin failed to laugh.

'Don't be facetious. How on earth did he come to believe that? Explain, please.'

Sighing heavily, Rachel looked meaningfully at her cousin. 'I'll give you three guesses where he was three years ago.'

Emma was quick on the uptake, and her chin dropped. 'You're not serious?'

'I've never been more so. He saw it all, Em. What's more, he believed everything he saw,' Rachel added, with an upsurge of anger as she recalled the moment he had told her. 'That's why he dislikes me so much.'

'But surely he's seen you're not really like that?' Emma pursued reasonably, and Rachel uttered a scoffing laugh.

'You'd think so, wouldn't you? But Nathan is a law unto himself. He believes there are two Rachels, and nothing I could say would convince him otherwise.'

'You tried, then?' Emma challenged suspiciously, and her cousin scowled.

'Of course I tried! He wouldn't have it. Besides,

he needs Rachel the man-eater to do his dirty work for him!'

'Oh, Lord, I don't like the sound of this. You'd better tell me everything, Rachel, right from the beginning,' Emma ordered, and listened with a growing unease at the tale that unfolded.

'So you see,' Rachel insisted when she came to the end of it, 'once he had said all that, I couldn't possibly refuse.'

Emma shook her head. 'You could, but, being you, you wouldn't. He made you mad, so it's a case of damn the torpedoes, you're going to prove him wrong.'

'You're darn right I am! What have I got to lose anyway? The man couldn't think worse of me.'

'No,' Emma agreed softly. 'But will he think better of you when you make a fool out of him?'

Rachel sat back with a grumpy sigh, not wanting to admit the truth of that. 'Probably not, but *I'll* feel better.' Remembering, her green eyes flashed angrily. 'He has no right to judge me like that.'

Emma, as usual, tried to pour oil on troubled waters. 'I know you're angry, and you have a right to be,' she added hastily, when Rachel made to interrupt. 'But do consider the consequences. You could be playing with fire.'

'Hah!' Rachel snorted. 'What can he possibly do?'

'Almost anything, I should imagine,' Emma murmured worriedly. 'What if he decides to get his own back and turns those big baby blues on you? Have you thought of that?'

She hadn't until then. The possibility sent shivers down her spine, and fear had very little to do with it. 'I can take care of myself,' she insisted.

'Come on, Rachel, you're in love with the man. You have been since the first time you met him. Like it or not, you're vulnerable, and that scares me. I don't want to see you get hurt, but I can't see any other outcome.'

Rachel's jaw took on a stubborn tilt. 'I can't back out now, Emma. There's more to it than just spitting in Nathan's eye. We're doing something for Grandfather, and no matter what happens I've still got to go to America with Nathan tomorrow.'

Faced with that, Emma sighed helplessly. 'Just be careful, OK? Make sure you keep a good distance from our Lothario. There's no need to hand yourself to him on a plate.'

'I promise I'll be careful,' Rachel replied, deciding it was advisable not to tell her cousin that her role was to be that of Nathan's latest lover. The argument that would produce would probably last all night, and end up with Emma not speaking to her.

'Famous last words,' Emma harrumphed with a shake of her head.

Rachel pulled a face, but there was nothing she could say to ease her cousin's fears. Only returning unscathed would do, and she was determined that that was how it would be.

'I'm sorry to have sprung this on you, but it was a surprise to me, too. With any luck we can get this thing sorted out over the weekend. Will you be able to manage till then?'

Emma couldn't stay mad for long, and nodded confidently. 'Sure. No problem. I'll have Annie with me, and Katrina said I could call on her any time, so don't worry about the business. Just get yourself back here in one piece.'

'You can count on it,' Rachel promised soberly, relieved that that hadn't gone too badly. Clambering to her feet, she held a hand out to Emma. 'Come and see what I've bought, and help me decide what else to take. Do you think I should wear that little black number I bought last year, or the green silk?'

Emma allowed herself to be pulled to her feet. 'Oh, the green. Most definitely the green,' she agreed with a wicked grin, and with a laugh Rachel led the way to her bedroom.

Emma insisted on driving Rachel to the airport the following day, despite the traffic. They had talked well into the night, and although Emma was far from happy she had eventually got into the mood and helped Rachel pack, even offering up some items of her own.

'Have you got everything?' Emma checked now, watching the porter remove the set of matching luggage from the boot of the car and stack it on a trolley.

'If I've forgotten anything it's too late now,' Rachel responded with a jaunty grin. She was looking forward to seeing Nathan's face when she waltzed in, as she had said to Emma more than once.

The idea had struck her around midnight or so, and had proved irresistible. A dumb blonde he wanted, so a dumb blonde he was getting.

Emma shook her head as she surveyed her cousin's appearance. 'He'll have a fit when he sees you,' she declared dryly, and Rachel burst into giggles.

'Oh, I do hope so!' she prayed.

She had her hair brushed out in a lush halo that bounced when she walked and felt decidedly odd, and her make-up was a tad less than subtle. Not garish, just…noticeable. As for her clothes… She wore one of those stretch skirts, which had shrunk in the wash and showed a heart-stopping length of thigh, and a vest top of Emma's which clung to her own slightly fuller figure.

'Well, will I do?' she asked, slipping on a pair of dark glasses and attempting to tug her skirt an inch or two lower. 'You don't think it's too OTT?'

Emma rolled her eyes. 'I can hear the wolf whistles already!' she commented wryly, then waved her hands in a shooing motion. 'Off you go. Best not keep him waiting. I'd love to be a fly on the wall when he sees you.'

'I promise to tell you all about it when I get back,' Rachel responded with another grin. 'Well, here goes!'

Slipping the strap of her bag onto her shoulder, Rachel claimed her vanity case from the trolley and took a deep breath. 'I'll ring you as soon as I can,' she promised, then quickly turned and led the way into the concourse.

Nathan had told her where he would meet her when he had telephoned before breakfast to check that she hadn't changed her mind, and, sure enough, there he was. Her heart did its usual little flip-flop. Lord, he was the best-looking man in the crowded hall, and the trousers and casual jacket he was wearing were so sexy she shivered in visceral response. She had been concentrating so hard on her own clothes, she had given no thought to what he would be wearing, and the possible effect it would have on her. The word 'lethal' sprang to mind, and she hastily bade her quaking heart be still.

Forging on, she was aware of the crowd shifting to make a path for her, and decided she knew how Moses had felt when he parted the Red Sea. Even at a distance she knew the instant Nathan spotted her, and swore she felt the tremor of shock which ripped through him at the sight of her.

Biting her lip to hold back a nervous giggle, Rachel swayed up to him, set her case at her feet and favoured him with a vacuous smile.

'Sorry, Darling, am I late? Have you been waiting long?' she asked brightly, ignoring the fact that he was looking at her with something close to volcanic rage.

Nathan ignored her questions in favour of one of his own. 'What in the name of creation are you wearing? Or I should say *almost* wearing?'

Her expression was the ultimate in uncomprehending disappointment. 'I thought you liked my legs, darling. Why, didn't you just say last night...?'

She got no further. A hand fastened like a vice

on her wrist, cutting off the words as his blue eyes narrowed dangerously. 'That's enough,' he ordered sharply, then turned to the grinning porter and handed over a note. 'Thanks. We'll take it from here,' he dismissed, and the man reluctantly walked away. Only then did Nathan turn back to Rachel. His expression was not encouraging. 'OK, what's the game? Why are you wearing those clothes?'

Rachel lifted one delicate eyebrow questioningly. 'Now, darling, you didn't expect me to turn up naked, did you?' she countered, at her dippiest, and watched that telltale nerve tick in his jaw. As a barometer of his irritation it was priceless.

'No, but I did expect you to turn up wearing something halfway decent,' he growled. 'You look...' His eyes travelled the length of her legs and back again, and she felt it like a lick of flame. Swallowing a lump which had appeared in her throat, she waited whilst he struggled to find the right word. 'Outrageous.'

Which was exactly what she had been aiming at. It was good to know she had hit the mark. She almost felt for him, but not enough to change her mind. 'I'll have you know this skirt cost me a small fortune.'

His grunt was decidedly uncomplimentary. 'You were robbed.'

Rachel very nearly spoilt it all by laughing, but that would never do. 'Well, there's no need to be nasty! I know it's a little short, but...'

'Short! Its almost indecent!'

She blinked once, twice, and suddenly there were

tears in her eyes. 'Don't be angry with me, darling. I thought you'd like it. I really did. Oh, Lord, I'm so dumb!' she half turned away, scrabbling in her bag for a tissue.

There followed a loaded silence.

'Talking of dumb, that makes two of us. *That* was quite a performance,' Nathan declared dryly, and Rachel laughed and turned round, her tears miraculously vanished.

He didn't look too amused, and her nerves jolted, but she kept her cool and made a play of patting her hair into place. 'Why, thank you. We aim to please,' she quipped back lightly.

Nathan picked up her case and handed it to her with an old-fashioned look. 'You certainly gave the male population of the airport a thrill. Did you enjoy yourself?'

Taking the vanity case, Rachel quirked an eyebrow at him. 'Does the male population include you?' she queried in her normal voice.

His lip curved mockingly. 'Sweetheart, you have legs any red-blooded male would want wrapped around him—providing he wasn't too choosy about the rest of you.'

The words stung, though doubtless he thought her skin too thick for her to feel anything. Still, she smiled, albeit thinly. 'You know, I don't think I've ever been insulted with so much finesse. You're gold medal standard, Nathan.'

It was his turn to affect a drawl. 'Why, thank you, darling. You just naturally bring out the best in me.'

The *beast* would be more accurate, in her opinion.

'You flatter me. You don't need any help at all. You're just naturally talented that way.'

He laughed huskily. 'Miaow. So, tell me, Rachel, why the act?'

She batted her lashes at him. 'I didn't want to let you down. Was I dumb enough for you?'

'You're forgetting. I'm not the one who likes dumb blondes. One thing's for sure, though. Ames won't miss you in that get-up. Come on, let check in your luggage.'

Rachel allowed herself to be steered to the check-in counter. 'You prefer intelligent blondes, do you?'

'My preferences aren't in question here. Ames is the one you have to turn on, not me. What did you do? Bring your whole wardrobe?' Nathan charged exasperatedly as he noted just how many cases she had with her.

Rachel watched with growing irritation as the check-in girl made eyes at Nathan despite her own presence at his side. She felt a sudden feline urge to scratch, and suppressed it with an effort. He wasn't hers, and she had no right to be jealous. On the other hand, the girl didn't know that, and on the spur of the moment Rachel slipped her arm through Nathan's and clung like a vine.

'I went shopping just for you, darling.'

Nathan looked from her to the clerk and back again. There was a gleam in his eye she didn't quite like. 'Is that so? Then I'll look forward to a fashion show later,' he murmured huskily, receiving their boarding passes with a smile of thanks. When they were relatively alone, he eased her grip on his arm.

'Cut it out, Rachel. The act doesn't need to start until we get there.'

Releasing him, she smoothed down her skirt. 'Practice makes perfect. May I remind you that you have a part to play too? It isn't all down to me. Just how good a gambler are you?'

He cast her a mocking glance. 'Doubting my ability, sweetheart?'

She shrugged. 'You know what they say. Lucky at love, unlucky at cards.'

That brought a grin to his face. 'Then we're OK on that score, for I've never been in love,' he told her, and she blinked at him in surprise.

'What...never? Despite all your women?'

He didn't look altogether pleased at that. 'You make it sound as if there have been hundreds.'

'I imagine there have been!' Rachel exclaimed disgustedly. If she put her mind to it, she was certain she could name at least fifty.

'You have one hell of an imagination, sweetheart. Try using it on Ames instead of my love life,' he advised caustically.

They had, by this time, reached the departure gate, and, their flight having been called, Rachel said nothing whilst they went through the motions of boarding the plane and settling into their seats. It wasn't until they were airborne and the seat belt light had gone off that she returned to the subject.

'So, what was wrong with all those women you've dated that you've never loved any of them?' she asked him curiously.

'They asked too many irritating questions,' he

countered sardonically, making himself comfortable and in the process giving Rachel a magnificent view of his leanly muscular legs. Her mouth went dry and she had to lick her lips to moisten them in order to respond.

'I'm just making conversation,' she said in a croaky voice, and his laugh was dry.

'Women never *just* do anything. There's always an ulterior motive,' he returned, turning his head and shooting her an assessing look.

She met it with a raised brow of her own. 'Really? And what would you say mine was?'

Entirely masculine lips curved into a far too enticing smile. 'I'm still working on it. I'll let you know when I've decided.'

She didn't think she liked the sound of that. 'I thought I was an open book to you.'

'Even open books can spring surprises. For instance, that perfume you're wearing is very sexy,' he told her out of the blue, and surprised colour bloomed in her cheeks.

'I'm not wearing perfume,' she corrected, without thinking, and then wished she'd kept quiet when she saw interest deepen the blue of his eyes. The silent question set her pulse rocketing. 'It's body lotion,' she admitted grudgingly.

'Very nice,' he murmured huskily, and tiny chills raced each other along her spine.

'Stop it,' she ordered, aggravated that, whilst her brain knew he was just playing with her, her senses responded with a will of their own. It was so galling.

The man had no real interest in her. It was all a game to him.

'Stop what?' Nathan asked lazily, though the glint in his eye told her he knew very well.

Rachel set her teeth, refusing to be charmed. 'There's no need to flirt with me here. We aren't on stage yet.'

Laughing, Nathan finally turned away from her. 'Like you, I'm just getting in a little practice, darling,' he taunted, neatly hoisting her with her own petard.

'Practice is the very last thing you need!' she sniped back. He was too good already.

She concentrated on the view out of the window until a stewardess offered her a magazine. She took it gratefully and buried her nose in it until the in-flight meal was served. After they had eaten, she lay back and closed her eyes. She had only intended to doze to while away the time, and it came as something of a shock to feel herself being shaken awake a long time later.

It was nothing to the jolt she got when she opened her eyes and found herself staring up into Nathan's handsome face. The bottom fell out of her stomach when her tiny intake of air drew in the tantalising scent of his aftershave. God, but he smelt good, and that was all her sleepily bemused mind could register in those first few vital seconds of wakefulness.

'We're going to be landing shortly,' he informed her, and the rumble of his voice echoing in her ear handed her yet another shock. Not only had she fallen asleep, but at some point during that time she had actually made herself comfortable by pillowing her head on his shoulder. That brought her sharply awake.

'Oh!' she exclaimed softly, sitting up in disarray, her cheeks turning a charming shade of pink. 'Sorry. You should have pushed me off.'

'You looked far too comfortable.'

'Maybe, but...'

Nathan reached across and brushed aside a stray lock of hair which had stuck to her cheek. 'I didn't mind you using me as a pillow.'

Rachel couldn't make up her mind if that made her feel better or worse. She did know she felt as if she had lost ground, and sought to make it up. 'I expect you're used to women falling asleep on you,' she retorted, a shade tartly, then could have cut her tongue out when she realised her words had a double meaning.

It wasn't lost on Nathan either, and he laughed easily. 'Well, now, that all depends who was on top, doesn't it?' he taunted, and Rachel instantly had such a vivid mental picture of two bodies locked in passion that she went hot all over.

'You're incorrigible! You know damn well I didn't mean that,' she said angrily, though the anger was directed at herself more than him, for not being able to control her thoughts.

'I do, but you would have said it if you'd thought of it. By the way, in case you're wondering, you don't snore. You snuffle a bit, but I found that kind of cute.'

That he didn't suffer a fatal wound was due entirely to the fact that a stewardess appeared beside them, reminding them to fasten their seat belts for landing. Rachel sat back and did her best to ignore him. Not easy when her whole body was still in a state of meltdown because she had snuggled up to him in her sleep. Then, of course, he had chosen to flirt with her again, and, boy, was he ever good at it. He didn't mean anything by it, it was all due to his perverted sense of humour, but it played havoc with her wayward senses.

How long had they been in close company? Just a few hours and already he was turning her inside out. The sooner they were on the ground and she could put some distance between them the better.

CHAPTER FOUR

THE Tahoe Caesar Hotel was an impressive struc-
ture, and although Rachel had stayed in many first-
class hotels in her travels she had to admit this was
in a class of its own. She was eternally thankful for
its air-conditioned coolness. The temperature outside
was bordering on the uncomfortable. Due to the difference in time zones, it was now early afternoon
here, the hottest part of the day. As she mounted the
lobby stairs she wished she hadn't chosen to wear
something so clingy. It had been fine for London,
where the temperature had been cooler, but here on
the west coast of America, it left her feeling limp.

Even Nathan had dispensed with his jacket and
unfastened the buttons of his shirt, giving her an
unexpected and tantalising glimpse of the silky dark
hair on his chest. It was hard to keep her mind off
it, let alone her eyes, and she was beginning to think
this whole trip had been devised as some sort of
punishment for deeds she couldn't remember doing.

Their suite, when they were shown to it, left her
speechless. It reminded her of something out of fair-
yland, and wasn't at all to her taste. Still, it had two
bedrooms, and that made up for a lot.

'Which room do you want?' she asked of Nathan
as soon as the bellboy had departed with a suitably
large tip. Unfortunately his departure only served to

64

make her uncomfortably aware that they were now alone in what could only be called intimate circumstances.

If Nathan was aware of it, it didn't faze him for an instant. 'You choose,' he responded, tossing his jacket over a chair and crossing to the impressively arrayed cocktail cabinet.

'I'll take the one on the right,' she decided, with a grimace at the less than scintillating conversation.

Nathan, though, didn't appear to find anything wrong. 'Fair enough. Do you want something to drink?'

'I'd kill for something cold and non-alcoholic,' she groaned, kicking off her shoes and dropping onto the nearest couch with a sigh of relief. 'Lord, but it's hot out there,' she puffed, lifting her hair away from her neck to allow some cooler air to touch her skin. It felt good.

'This will make you feel better,' Nathan declared from right beside her.

Rachel jumped and glanced up quickly, realising the thickness of the carpet had masked the sound of his approach. He was holding out a tall glass that was already beginning to frost with condensation.

She took it, unconsciously licking her lips at the thought of the cool liquid sliding down her parched throat. 'Thanks,' she sighed gratefully.

Nathan took the seat opposite her and raised his glass. Rachel found herself watching hypnotically as he took a long swig of his own drink. With his head back, she could see each swallow straining the sweat-dampened skin of his throat, and suddenly her own was closing on an upsurge of desire. A bead of sweat tracked into the dark nest of curls just visible above his shirt and she experienced an intense longing to follow the path it had taken with her lips. All at once her blood seemed to flow thickly through her veins and she stifled a groan way down deep in her throat.

'Keep looking at me like that, sweetheart, and I'll start to think you're planning on having me for supper instead of food.' Nathan's husky observation brought her eyes up to his, to find him watching her with a strange gleam in his eyes.

Her body rippled with the shock of being discovered in a display of such blatantly sensual interest. Oh, Lord, she was losing her grip, she thought despairingly. Knowing she couldn't say he was mistaken, her only recourse was to bluff her way out.

'I was just window-shopping. Don't worry, you'd be too rich for me,' she drawled, with all the sangfroid at her disposal, and saw his lips curve in wry amusement.

'Yeah, I've noticed you tend to go for blander meat. You might be able to control it better, but I doubt very much if it really satisfies your appetite,' he returned sardonically, downing the rest of his drink and setting the glass aside.

He was right, of course, but for all the wrong reasons. She knew the only man who would satisfy her both emotionally and physically sat watching her across a few feet of carpet. However, as she had every reason to suppose that that would never happen, it didn't do to dwell on the subject.

'I have no complaints,' she replied, with a faint shrug of the shoulders to signify her lack of care.

Nathan's lips twitched and his expression grew sceptical. 'So you're not hankering after something you can never have?'

Rachel tipped her head on one side and smiled secretively. 'You know what they say. Never say never. The words could come back to haunt you.'

'Oh, I'll risk it,' he countered smoothly, and they stared at each other for a long moment before Rachel relaxed back into her seat and took a much needed sip of her drink.

'So, when does this fiasco get underway?' she asked, changing the subject, safe in the knowledge that she had successfully managed damage limitation this time.

Nathan crossed one leg over the other, casually grasping its ankle in one hand. 'Tonight. It's lucky you slept for most of the flight—hopefully you shouldn't feel too jetlagged later on. I'll get Room Service to bring you a light meal, and then you should try to catch a few more hours' sleep this afternoon—that's what I'll be doing. As for our plan of action, according to Linus's sources Luther Ames has booked a table in the main restaurant here for a large dinner party. From there, if he follows his usual plan—and I see no reason why he shouldn't— the whole party will move into the casino.'

'That's when we make our move?' She sought confirmation, unable to shake off the feeling she was descending into some sort of forties *film noir* gangster movie for which she was totally unsuited.

Nathan nodded. 'Apparently his current game of choice is baccarat. He likes nothing more than to set up a bank and take on all comers. Of course, it helps if you can afford to lose, which he can. Nobody knows the actual extent of his personal fortune.'

Rachel instantly saw a flaw in the plan. 'Never mind him. Can *you* afford to lose?' she queried in genuine concern. It was one thing to try and recover the letters, and quite another for Nathan to lose a fortune in the attempt.

He sent her a steady look. 'I don't intend to.'

She raised an eyebrow sceptically at his confidence. 'I imagine most gamblers have the same certainty, and look what happens to them.'

A smile slowly curved his lips. 'You're forgetting. I'm lucky at cards. Always have been.'

Rachel snapped her fingers. 'That's right. It's love you know nothing about. I'll have to keep praying that you don't suddenly fall head over heels in the next few days. I'd hate to see you bankrupt yourself.'

'That,' he declared dryly, getting to his feet, 'will never happen.'

Rachel followed suit. 'Not whilst you're happy playing the field, at any rate,' she responded sardonically.

Picking up his glass, he carried it over to the bar and refilled it. 'Then it's going to be up to you, sweetheart. I'll hook him....all you have to do is land him,' Nathan declared, and she could swear she heard him laughing under his breath as he disap-

peared into his bedroom, closing the door behind
him.

Damn him, she cursed silently, going to her own
bedroom and shutting the door with more force than
was strictly necessary. Let him laugh now, for the
last laugh would be hers. Crossing to the bed, she
deftly unfastened the largest case and drew out of it
the shimmering green evening dress she would wear
that night. It was supposed to be travel-proof, but
she put it on a hanger and left it in the bathroom so
that when she showered later the steam would remove any tiny wrinkles.

She unpacked the remainder of her clothes
quickly. Not that there were too many of them, despite appearances. The cases had been for show. She
guessed that the type of blonde Ames preferred
would always take her wardrobe with her. It would,
after all, be the tool of her trade. A trade she knew
nothing of and yet was expected to use to keep
Luther Ames otherwise engaged.

Rachel plopped down onto the edge of the bed
and chewed on her lip a little worriedly. It was one
thing to play the dumb blonde with Nathan, and
quite another to deliberately entice Luther Ames, using promises she had no intention of following
through with. Especially as she didn't like the sound
of him one little bit. She acknowledged that she had
been quite deliberately ignoring this particular aspect of their trip.

As a rule she enjoyed flirting. Sometimes it was
just to tease old friends, and at others it was part of
the dating ritual. She had never practised it with se-

rious intent. Flirting was simply an enjoyable pas-
time. To do it in cold blood, with the full intention
of gaining the attention of a man she knew to be at
the very least a blackmailer, made her shiver. Yet
she had agreed, albeit by use of devious methods,
to help. Lord, she just hoped she was up to it. She
would hate to let Linus down.

Nathan would never let her forget it either. Which
was, ironically, all the spur she needed to do her
utmost to pull it off. She had a reputation—an er-
roneous one, as it turned out—to keep up. A clever
woman could keep a man hooked yet at arm's length
for as long as she wanted, and she had always considered herself a very clever woman. Except for the
error of falling for Nathan Wade, but everyone was
allowed one mistake, weren't they?

A knock at the door heralded the arrival of Room
Service, as Nathan had promised, bearing a light,
perfectly cooked omelette and a salad. After clearing
her plate, Rachel decided to take Nathan's advice
and have another few hour's sleep before preparing
for the evening ahead. She had a feeling she was
going to need all her wits about her.

When Rachel awoke she felt a great deal better, and
a glance at her watch told her it was time to get
ready for her first full performance. Wanting to take
full advantage of her magnificent *ensuite* bathroom,
she chose to have a long, relaxing bath and hair
wash instead of the swift shower she had been planning on. Three quarters of an hour later she climbed
out of the cooling water, wrapped herself in a lux-

urious bath sheet and padded back into her bedroom. She had no idea what Nathan was doing. She hadn't heard a sound from outside since he had disappeared into his room. Shrugging, she searched out the hair-dryer and set to work on her hair.

Knowing how important first impressions were, more so in this case, she spent a great deal of time over her appearance. Her hair, once dry, was a lush golden halo about her head and shoulders. Subtle application of make-up made her eyes look enor-mous, whilst giving her lips an extra fullness. Underwear came next. The dress did not allow the wearing of a bra, but she chose panties and sus-pender belt that were the merest breath of satin and lace. After carefully drawing on the finest denier stockings, she stepped into the dress. It fitted like a dream, the tiny straps hardly seeming strong enough to hold the bodice up. Only when she had placed matching shoes on her feet did she turn and look in the mirror.

Rachel was used to seeing herself this way, but even she was amazed by the results. She seemed to shimmer and glow. Her heart-rate increased. If this didn't knock Nathan dead, she didn't know what would, she thought, and realised with a lurch of her stomach that behind the need to dress up for the part she was playing there was a stronger element. She wanted to make an impression on Nathan. Crazy though the idea was, she couldn't help it. She just wanted to see something other than disdain flare in his eyes. It could be over in seconds, but if she saw it...

Impatiently she told herself not to be so foolish. There would be nothing to see. He disliked her. Never for a second had he hinted otherwise. She had to get real.

A sharp rap on the door made her nerves jump.

'Yes? What is it?' she called out just a little breathlessly.

'Are you about done in there? I've a table booked for eight-thirty,' Nathan informed her, and she took a swift glance at her watch. Ten minutes. A ball of panicky excitement settled in her stomach. Showtime.

'Oh, OK, I'll be right with you,' she called out, casting a rapid eye around the room to make sure she had forgotten nothing. If she had, it was too late now. She grimaced as she picked up her evening purse from the bed.

Taking a deep breath, she crossed to the door and unlocked it. When she stepped into the lounge, Nathan was standing at the bar. At the sound of the door opening he turned, the glass he had filled freezing halfway to his mouth.

The arrested look in his blue eyes was everything Rachel had been hoping for. But the sudden fire which flared to life in the depths of them, even though it was quickly extinguished, was a bonus. Her nerves jolted. She recognised desire when she saw it, and for the briefest moment his expression had revealed a scorching amount of it. Dear Lord, he was attracted to her! It was staggering to realise that, no matter what he said, his eyes had just told her quite another story. Clearly he didn't *want* to be

attracted, and she knew why. He didn't want to want
the woman he thought her to be, but she wasn't that
woman. The question was, what was she going to
do about it? She needed to think, but there was no
time now. All she could do was hug to herself the
knowledge of what he had given away.

'Here I am. Will I do, do you think?' she asked
huskily, walking into the room and giving a twirl.

After the merest pause, Nathan downed his drink
and set the glass aside. 'If you don't, Ames will be
a damned hard man to please,' he declared dryly as
he advanced towards her. 'You've pulled out all the
stops, I see.'

Disappointment settled like a lead weight in her
stomach. Yes, she had seen desire flare in his eyes
when he saw her, but he was not going to act upon
it. His words told her quite clearly that he was not
about to let his body overrule his brain. She was a
means to an end, that was all. It hurt, but she refused
to be crushed by it because she knew he felt something now. She raised her chin, knowing that if she
wanted any sort of relationship with this man she
would have to overcome his steely self-control. A
daunting prospect, but one she would not be afraid
to take on. For now, though, she had to bide her
time.

'I decided I needed to make an instant impression,' she explained with a shrug. 'After all, we are
pushed for time.'

Nathan halted mere inches away, his eyes holding
hers. 'Just remember you're doing this for Linus, not

yourself. Don't try adding Ames to your list of conquests.'

She was sorely tempted to hit him for even suggesting it. If he only knew there was but one man she wanted to conquer. She shot him a coy look, knowing she was going to have her work cut out for her, but, strangely enough, the character he disliked would give her the cover she needed to do some elementary groundwork. There was no time like the present.

Reaching out, she stroked her palm along his lapel soothingly. 'Now, there's no need to be jealous, darling. You know you're the only man I care about!' she exclaimed in the clinging tones of a seductress. If only he knew how true it was!

As she'd expected, Nathan took an irritated breath, but a nerve ticked away in his jaw. He wasn't as cool as he looked. 'I never waste time being jealous,' he retorted, brushing her hand away.

'Of course not,' Rachel concurred with a faint curve of her lip, whilst her palm still felt the heat of his body. No, not cool at all. 'There are so many other women just waiting in the wings for you. Poor deluded fools.'

'Now who sounds jealous, darling?' he came back silkily. 'Could it be that secretly you want to be one of those poor deluded fools?' he taunted, and, because it was true, she made herself laugh lightly.

'I'd sooner be nibbled to death by ducks,' she lied, and had the heart-squeezing pleasure of seeing amusement dance in those fascinating blue eyes.

'My thoughts exactly at the notion of getting

mixed up with you. It's amazing how much we do agree on.'

'Amazing,' she agreed with heavy irony. They wanted each other, too, but that was something he wasn't ready to discuss. In fact, if she hadn't seen his unwanted attraction with her own eyes she would have had a hard time believing it existed, so good was he at hiding his feelings. She had to hide hers too. 'Well, what now?'

'Now we go down to dinner. But first...' He reached into the pocket of his dinner jacket and pulled out something that flashed fire and ice.

Rachel's breath caught as he held up an exquisite diamond necklace. Automatically her hand went to her throat. She had been joking about the diamonds, but apparently he had taken her seriously. As ever, she felt the cynicism of his notion of her like a wound in her heart. One day she might change that, for she had hope now. Faint, but persistent.

'Turn round,' he ordered, and though she wanted to protest she did as he bade her, shivering as the gems settled on her flesh. For a moment she felt the brush of his fingers as he dealt with the clasp, then he moved away and she sighed heavily before facing him again.

Stepping back slightly, Nathan ran his eyes over her in a lazy inspection which missed nothing and, try though she might to stop it, set all the fine hairs on her body standing to attention. 'You look stunning,' he pronounced finally.

There was a flicker of warmth in his eyes, and, had things been different, with that tiny piece of encouragement she would have been in his arms. However, it wasn't so, and Rachel cleared her throat hastily, struggling for composure. 'Stunning enough to get Ames's attention?'

The smile that set hearts tripping all over the universe appeared, and had the same effect on Rachel. 'A man would have to be made of stone not to notice you tonight. You'll be the most beautiful woman there.'

An hour ago she would have thought the compliment mere window-dressing words, but her newly discovered knowledge told her he meant it. She wasn't supposed to know that, though. He would close down tighter than a clam if he suspected she'd guessed his secret. For now the status quo had to be maintained. With that in mind Rachel licked dry lips and willed her pulse to settle down. She had to respond in kind.

'Don't go overboard. This is still me, you know,' she told him mockingly.

He quirked an eyebrow at her. 'Ah, but this is a very beautiful you, and I've always believed that beauty should be acknowledged,' he informed her in a soft, warm voice which turned her stomach over.

Cool it, Rachel, she instructed herself firmly. This man is a master of the art of flirtation. And she knew that if he ever did use it on her with serious intent, remote though the likelihood was right now, she would be lost.

'It's only fair to warn you, Nathan, that if you

keep saying things like that you'll turn my head,' she warned sardonically.

His lips twitched. 'Vanity is something I would never accuse you of,' he countered seductively, and she blinked in exaggerated surprise.

'Why not?' she challenged drolly. 'You've accused me of nearly everything else!'

'A fact that doesn't appear to trouble you unduly,' Nathan observed with a mocking gleam in his eye.

Rachel held that gaze with a stoical one of her own. 'I never waste my time protesting to deaf ears.'

'Meaning I don't listen?'

'Meaning you *won't* listen. A small but significant difference.'

His laugh was so blatantly sexy it made her shiver. 'On the contrary, I always listen to what a woman wants. It's my pleasure to give her pleasure.'

Rachel's throat closed over as she followed his meaning only too well. 'That isn't quite what I meant,' she protested a trifle faintly. 'But it doesn't surprise me at all that you would wilfully misunderstand.'

Nathan's lips twitched again. 'I enjoy teasing women. It's all part of the game.'

'Maybe, but I'm not part of that game. Emma was right. No woman is safe from you! You're even flirting with *me*, and I know how much you dislike me.' It would have been expecting a lot for him to deny her statement, and it was no surprise that he didn't.

'Emma?'

Too late she realised she hadn't meant to mention her cousin in case Nathan knew enough to make the link. She improvised hastily. 'My…business partner. She thinks I'm out of my mind going anywhere with you.'

'Whereas you know you're safer with me than with practically any other man you could name,' he returned succinctly, giving her heart another painful twist.

'Which is exactly what I told her,' she confirmed, instinctively protecting herself. 'Shall we go?'

Nathan smiled faintly. 'Does it irk you that I'm not interested in you, Rachel? Were you hoping to sharpen your claws on me?' he taunted as he took her elbow and urged her to the door.

Rachel felt his touch like a lick of flame, sending tiny shock waves over her flesh, but she was too sensible to jerk away. 'I might do it yet, so I wouldn't crow too soon, Nathan darling,' she warned daringly, following the time-honoured principle that attack is often the best form of defence.

'My, but you do love to live dangerously, sweetheart.'

She sent him a sweet smile over her shoulder. 'Of course. But that's why you picked me for the job. You can't start complaining now.'

He grinned at her and pressed the lift button. 'I'm not complaining. In fact, this is turning out to be more amusing than I expected.'

The lift arrived and they stepped inside. 'Funny, I was thinking the same thing myself. You were right; we do have more in common than you think.'

They reached the ground in something short of a nanosecond and walked out into a busy foyer. 'Just don't forget that once this is over you and I will be back on opposite sides of the fence,' he reminded her unnecessarily.

She laughed wryly. Maybe. Maybe not. 'If I do, I feel sure you'll remind me,' she retorted smartly, and felt rather than saw him smile as they walked along side by side.

'Count on it.'

The restaurant was busy at this time of night, and they had a short wait before being shown to their table.

'Have you ever met Luther Ames?' Rachel asked once they were seated and had been supplied with drinks.

'No, but I know him by sight,' Nathan answered, glancing casually around the crowded dining room. 'He isn't here yet.'

Rachel sipped at a glass of white wine. Though she could do with the bolster of strong drink, she knew she needed to keep a clear head for what she had to do. 'Will he have heard of you, do you think?' It was a possibility she hadn't considered before. If Ames knew anything about Nathan, they would be sunk before they started.

'Not that I'm aware of,' Nathan answered unconcernedly. 'There's no reason why he should know of me. Even if he does, I doubt he would make the connection between Linus and his aunt. We'll just have to play it by ear and hope for the best.'

They were waiting for the arrival of their first course when a shift in the noise level drew their and almost every other diner's attention to the entrance.

A tall, dark haired, handsome man in his early forties, dressed in white dinner jacket, frilled shirt and black bow tie, stood in the van of a chattering group of people, all elegantly dressed and showing visible signs of wealth.

Rachel glanced back at Nathan and shivered when she saw the grim set of his jaw and the icy look in his eyes. She barely needed to ask the question, but voiced it anyway. 'Is that him?'

'In the flesh,' Nathan confirmed coldly, without taking his eyes off Ames.

Rachel followed his gaze back to the broadly smiling man who was now being shown to where a large table stood empty. 'He looks harmless enough,' she remarked inanely, watching the progression of the entourage.

Nathan's lips curled derisively as he turned his attention back to her. 'If he looked like the black-hearted snake we know him to be, nobody would trust him. He's nobody's fool, Rachel. Remember that.'

'Oh, I will,' she concurred, and the promise was heartfelt. She trusted both her grandfather's and Nathan's judgement too well to ignore it. But what was sauce for the goose... 'Just make sure you remember it too,' she advised him, bringing a surprised look to his face.

'Worried about me, sweetheart?' he teased, and she shrugged to hide her very real concern.

'I wouldn't like to have to explain your sudden demise to Grandfather,' she said dryly, making him laugh softly.

'And there I was beginning to think you cared. I'm shattered.'

She gave him a look. 'You look like it.'

'You're a hard woman, but I know several ways to soften steel.'

Rachel uttered a soft laugh. 'Oh, I just bet you do!'

Nathan turned his attention back to Luther Ames. The group had been seated and, from the loud laughter, were already well lubricated. 'There's no point in making a move now. We'll wait until they head for the gaming rooms.' Turning back to her, he noticed her suddenly pale cheeks. 'Are you all right?'

She pressed a hand to her stomach. 'I think I just lost my appetite,' she said jokingly, though nerves were making her stomach do an uncomfortable dance inside. Much to her surprise, Nathan reached across the table and gave her other hand a squeeze.

'You'll be fine. Just remember you aren't on your own. I'll be there to help you if things turn nasty.'

'Specify ''nasty'',' she quipped with a grimace. 'It's a very loose term.'

Nathan stared at her seriously. 'I won't let anything happen to you, darling. Trust me on that, if on nothing else.'

She did. There was no question of it. 'I suppose there isn't time to change my mind?' She made a poor attempt at a joke, but he grinned.

'Rachel Shaw doesn't renege on a deal. Linus told me that himself.'

She blinked in surprise, though her grandfather's

confidence in her did her a power of good. 'He did, huh?'

He nodded. 'Cross my heart and—'

'Don't finish that!' she ordered hastily, holding up her hand. 'There are certain things I don't even want to think about.'

Nathan took hold of her hand and ran his thumb backwards and forwards over it soothingly. 'The man's slime, but so far as we know he's never done anything requiring a life sentence.'

Rachel sniffed. 'Let's hope he doesn't undergo a radical change of direction on our behalf!' she retorted smartly, and Nathan laughed huskily.

'At least you haven't lost your sense of humour,' he remarked dryly, and she slitted her eyes at him.

'Give me a few minutes and it will go. Trust me.'

Nathan tipped his head on one side quizzically. 'What's this all about, Rachel? I doubt very much if you have a nervous bone in your entire body.'

Little did he know. She could succumb to nerves like the next woman, only he thought of her as some sort of creature devoid of human emotions. She sighed and smiled coquettishly. 'Maybe I just wanted you to hold my hand, sweetie,' she returned, and wasn't at all surprised that he released her immediately.

'You're full of tricks today. First the tears, now this. What else is on the agenda?'

Rachel shook her head. 'That would be telling. I can't give away all my secrets at once, you know. A girl has to have some mystery.'

'Which is how I know you can do this standing on your head,' he observed calmly.

'Don't credit me with too much. I think I'd better try it the right way up first. Why make things difficult for myself?' she returned smartly as their food arrived. It looked and smelled delicious, and she felt her appetite returning. The momentary collywobbles were over. 'As soon as I get this food inside me I'll be ready for anything,' she promised brightly, not waiting for an invitation to tuck in.

All through the meal they were very much aware of the Luther Ames party not so very far away. The noise level rose from their table as the wine flowed, and everyone appeared to be having a good time. From the little Rachel could see, though, Ames himself drank very little. It gave her a small insight into the man. He liked to keep a clear head, so that he was always in control of the situation.

Almost two hours passed before Ames and his friends left the restaurant in search of the gaming rooms. Nathan allowed them ten minutes' grace before he looked over at Rachel.

'Ready?'

She took a steadying breath and squared her shoulders. She was Rachel the man-eater, capable of anything, remember. 'Lead me to him,' she responded confidently, and Nathan rose and walked round to help her up.

'I could almost feel sorry for the man. He doesn't know what's about to hit him,' he observed dryly, taking her elbow and steering her through the tables to the exit.

Rachel's grimace went unnoticed. Nathan might not be so confident if he knew her better, but if she pulled this off at least she would have his respect. It was all she could genuinely hope for.

CHAPTER FIVE

THEY HAD no difficulty finding Luther Ames, even though the rooms were thronged with people. Rachel had never seen the point of gambling, especially when the odds must always be with the house. OK, so people were winning, but the percentage was nowhere near that of the numbers who lost. Watching these people looking for answers they would never find here made her feel sad and angry, and left her with no inclination to try her hand.

The baccarat tables were surrounded by onlookers all eager to watch fortunes change hands. True to reports, Ames had a bevy of beauties about him. As banker, he had the shoe, and was deftly dealing the cards as they approached. On the way in Nathan had bought chips of a value which had taken Rachel's breath away. She couldn't believe he was actually going to bet such a sum, but with a casualness she could only admire Nathan took a vacant seat and set up his chips. Seeing them, Ames gave him a long, considering look, then proceeded to deal another round.

Rachel took a position behind Nathan, one hand resting possessively on his shoulder, and watched the run of play. Nathan lost that time, and, slipping into her role, she uttered an audible gasp.

'Oh, darling, you lost!' She pouted in disappointment. Looking up, she found Luther Ames staring at her. There was blatant sexual appreciation in his eyes and, though she disliked it, she eyed him in return and then sent him her best sultry smile. The response was instantaneous. He smiled back, and ran those eyes over her in a way that stripped her naked and left her feeling sullied.

Promising herself a long, cleansing shower when she got back to her room, she instinctively smoothed her hands over Nathan's shoulders. Under her fingers she felt Nathan flex his muscles, and knew he was nowhere near as relaxed as he appeared. She doubted if another soul in the room knew it. No wonder he had hidden his attraction to her for so long. He was the master of cool.

Nathan paid up and the play went on; he lost again, but on the third attempt he won handsomely. Rachel gave a whoop of delight and coiled her arms round Nathan's neck in a hug. 'I thought you were never going to win!' she whispered, for his ears only, kissing his cheek enthusiastically, leaving a smudge of lipstick behind.

Nathan grinned up at her. 'You and me both,' he admitted under his breath, then added more audibly, 'I told you you were my lucky mascot, darling. You just stay right there and bring me some more luck,' he ordered, and Rachel preened at his praise, brushing another kiss near his ear.

'If the eyes are supposed to be the mirror of the soul, this man's soul is a cesspool,' she added in an undertone, then straightened, smoothing her dress down over her hips. In doing so she managed to catch a glimpse of Ames watching her fixedly. She would say she had most certainly caught his attention.

'The lady is not only lucky, but beautiful too,' Luther Ames declared fulsomely from across the table, and she batted her eyes at him, producing her most dazzling smile.

'Why, thank you, sir. You are most gallant,' she responded, and was a little surprised to feel Nathan tense beneath her touch.

Ames grinned and paid off the winners and the game went on again. The right hand chair eventually became empty and Nathan moved into it, immediately calling banco. Ames stared at him narrowly.

'The bank stands at...' He named a figure that drained the strength from Rachel's knees, and she was glad she was holding on to Nathan. How he could sit there so calmly she couldn't imagine; her heart was thundering.

A hush fell as Ames dealt the cards, followed by a collected holding of breath as it became clear that Nathan held a natural. Unless Ames could match it, he would lose. For a full ten seconds it seemed as if the room had gone into slow motion as Ames revealed his cards, added another...and lost. Then pandemonium broke out. As laughter echoed round the onlookers Rachel drew in a shaky breath and looked at Ames. He was smiling, but even in the low lighting she could see it didn't quite reach his eyes.

'Congratulations, Mr...?'

'Wade. Nathan Wade,' Nathan supplied.

'You were lucky, Mr. Wade,' Ames declared, pushing over a stack of chips to cover the bet. 'I admire a man who is not afraid to take a risk. However you must allow me the opportunity to win this back.'

Nathan gathered up the chips and pocketed them. 'It would be my pleasure,' he agreed. 'However, not this evening. Tonight my lucky mascot and I intend to celebrate in style,' he went on as he rose to his feet and slipped his arm about Rachel's waist. With a nod to Ames he urged her away from the table. 'Come along, darling. You and I have some serious celebrating to do.'

'My God,' Rachel declared as soon as they were out of earshot. 'Do you know how much money you stood to lose?'

'Don't remind me,' Nathan said wryly.

Rachel groaned and placed a hand over her still racing heart. 'I almost died when he turned over that last card. Did you see his face? He didn't like losing, not one little bit.'

Nathan grinned down at her, and there was more than a hint of grim satisfaction in his eyes. 'I know. The man is not a good loser. He won't rest until he's won the money back. I fully intend to give him the chance.'

'Then why are we leaving?' she queried reasonably.

'Because I don't want to play in here. We need to be invited to his house, remember. If he's as sore a loser as he looked, the invitation won't be long in coming,' Nathan explained, making for the cashier to cash in his chips. When that was done they left the casino for the adjacent showroom.

They were shown to a table near the stage, and, keeping up the image, Nathan ordered champagne. When it arrived, Rachel took a much needed sip to steady herself. She wasn't cut out to be a gambler. She couldn't stand the tension.

'What are you going to do with the money?' She asked curiously some time later, and Nathan shot her a contemplative look.

'Hoping to do a little shopping, are you?' He ventured mockingly, and it annoyed her so much that she bit back her intended suggestion that he donate it to charity and produced a feline smile.

'We—ell, now you come to mention it, there are one or two things I've had my eye on for some time,' she purred, and wasn't surprised to see his eyes glaze over. Mr Predictability! 'For instance…'

'Forget it sweetheart. You aren't going to get your sticky fingers on one red cent of it,' he told her coolly, and she shook her head sadly.

'Tut, tut, it's rude to interrupt. Now you don't know what I was going to suggest,' she chastised him, and his lips curved in amusement.

'I can imagine,' he drawled scornfully, and it was all she could do to hide her sense of injustice. He never gave an inch. Never gave her the benefit of the doubt. It was so galling.

'You seem to *imagine* quite a lot of things about me. Do you know something? I think you think about me much more than you dare to admit,' she returned with a silky suggestiveness designed to set his back up. Unfortunately it missed the mark, and he turned it neatly back on her.

'I think about you all the time, sweetheart. It's the only way to keep one step ahead of you,' he countered smoothly, and she hid her frustration behind a cool smile.

'Surely that only works if you know where I'm going,' she pointed out dulcetly, and the hairs rose on her skin as she witnessed that fascinating gleam enter his eyes.

'Don't think I don't. There isn't a move you could make that I can't anticipate,' he returned equally softly.

There was, she realised, something dangerously exciting about bantering words with him in this fashion, despite the way he constantly taunted her, and it made her blood zing a little faster through her veins. 'That's quite a claim,' she said with a husky thread to her voice, and it made his lips curve, producing the dimple she secretly longed to touch.

'Not really. Women hold few mysteries for me. I doubt you know any tricks that would really surprise me.'

Rachel dropped her gaze to her glass, hating to be reminded of all the women he had known. He thought she was angling to be one of them, but she wasn't. What she wanted was to be the only one, but right now she had more chance of winning the lottery than of achieving that goal. However, that need not stop her picking away at the edges of his defences, so she looked up at him boldly.

'You won't know unless you try me,' she invited seductively, and held her breath for his reply.

It came with a wry laugh. 'You don't give up, do you?'

Curse it, but she loved the way he laughed. Life could be so unfair. 'What else is there to do?' she shrugged. 'I have to amuse myself somehow.'

He raised his glass and took a sip, eyeing her over it. 'I amuse you, do I?'

'You could do more than amuse me, only you're too scared,' she charged daringly, and his eyes narrowed speculatively.

'Is that so?'

'Um-hum,' she confirmed, allowing her eyes to rove over him in a way that set her heart tripping like fury. 'You're scared you might like it.'

Blue eyes glittered with amusement, and something else she couldn't put a name to. 'I am?'

'Oh, yes.' She nodded with a secretive smile, wondering what she would do if he suddenly took up the challenge. But then again, she knew he wouldn't. 'What price everything you've said if you plunge in and find yourself out of your depth?'

'I'm a strong swimmer. I never get out of my depth,' he advised her in the same light tone she was using.

Rachel wagged a finger at him. 'There you go again with that "never". I've told you before how dangerous it is to use it. You're taking an awfully big risk.'

He smiled faintly. 'A calculated risk, maybe, with the odds on my side.'

She shook her head in part-feigned, part-real annoyance at his attitude. 'It's possible to be over-confident. You're going to fall one day, and fall hard.'

Nathan looked at her squarely. 'Very likely, but it won't be for you, sweetheart. So disabuse yourself of that notion.'

It hurt to hear him say it so bluntly, but she didn't allow it to show even for an instant. 'It never entered my head,' she lied without compunction.

'I don't suppose it did. For all your faults, you're a sensible woman. You know what side your bread is buttered.'

Yes, the side that hit the ground! 'You'll turn my head with all this flattery.' she drawled mockingly, and waited expectantly for a pithy reply, but Nathan's attention had been caught by something beyond her. 'What is it?'

'Ames just walked in. No, don't look round,' he ordered sharply when he saw her about to do just that.

Rachel froze and licked her lips nervously. 'Has he seen us?'

Nathan shook his head. 'Not yet. Ah, now he has. Get ready, Rachel, he's heading our way.'

Rachel felt Luther Ames's presence before he arrived at their table. The man had an aura about him which set her teeth on edge. It was the most uncomfortable feeling she had ever experienced.

'Ah, Mr Wade, I'm delighted to find you still here,' Ames began as he came alongside, smiling in a way designed to impress them with his friendliness. It would have worked if they had been ignorant of his misdeeds. 'I was remiss in not making myself known to you before. Allow me to do so now. Luther Ames,' he introduced himself, holding out his hand.

Nathan shook it, then coolly slipped an arm round Rachel's shoulders. It felt for all the world as if he were laying claim to her, but she told her whimsical heart not to be so fanciful. It was all part of the act.

'What can I do for you, Mr Ames?' hr queried in equally friendly tones.

Rachel was uncomfortably aware that Luther Ames eyes had followed Nathan's possessive movement and were focused on her soft flesh. She was relieved when he drew them away to answer Nathan's question.

'Ah, I'll come to that in a moment. First, won't you introduced me to your lovely lady?' he said with a light laugh, but his eyes were hot when they returned to her.

Nathan glanced down at her, his look caressing. 'My lovely lady goes by the name of Rachel,' he revealed. 'Say hello to Mr Ames darling.'

'Hello, Mr Ames,' she responded obediently, smiling archly and holding out her hand. His hand felt uncomfortably damp when it closed around hers.

'Rachel.' Ames allowed her name to linger on his tongue, as if savouring it. 'An exquisite name for an exquisite woman,' he added, and she very nearly gagged at the flowery compliment.

Keeping her smile in place with an effort, Rachel drew her hand away slowly. 'You shouldn't be say-

ing such things, you know. You'll be making
Nathan jealous,' she exclaimed with a husky laugh,
giving Nathan a sideways look.

'As I said before, you're a very lucky man, Mr
Wade.'

'I believe so, Mr Ames,' Nathan responded dryly.
'With women and cards,' he added for good mea-
sure, which brought Luther Ames back to the point
of his presence there.

'As you say. But luck is a fickle mistress. You
must allow me the chance to turn lady luck in my
favour.'

Nathan inclined his head. 'Happy to. I'll be here
for a few more days. How do you say we meet tomorrow, or maybe the next night?'

Ames spread his hands. 'Alas, I am only here for
one night… You cannot see your way clear to…?'
He left the suggestion hanging, and Nathan shook
his head emphatically.

'I'm afraid not.'

'Then it seems I am out of luck, unless…' Ames
appeared to hesitate, but Rachel could see the cal-
culation in his eyes.

'Unless?' Nathan prompted, as he was expected
to.

Ames smiled, including Rachel in his supposed
warmth. 'Could I persuade you to be my guests for
a few more days? I have a house on the lake up by
Crystal Bay. I have some friends staying with me,
but not enough to make up a table, so I would be
pleased to have your company. The house is totally
secluded, with its own private beach. We will be

undisturbed. I can promise you you won't be disappointed.'

Nathan gave the appearance of uncertainty. 'I don't know. It sounds good, but Rachel was looking forward to doing some shopping. What do you say, sweetheart? Shall we go?'

Rachel reached out and ran her finger lightly over his lips. 'I'll go wherever you want me to, darling, you know that,' she sighed seductively.

Nathan closed his hand around hers and brought her palm to his lips. The brush of the caress sent a thrill through her whole body, even though she knew it was all for show. 'Then that's settled,' he said, turning back to Ames. 'We'll be happy to join you, Mr Ames.'

Ames's delight was scarcely hidden as he rubbed his hands together. 'Good. *Good.* I'll send a limousine for you in the morning.'

'No need. We have our own transport.' Nathan refused the offer politely.

'In that case I'll leave directions at the desk. I'll look forward to seeing you for lunch, Mr Wade, and you too, of course, Rachel.'

Nathan didn't release Rachel until Ames left the room. 'Well, sweetheart, for good or bad, we're in,' he stated with satisfaction. 'The next part won't be so easy.'

Rachel curled her fingers about her still tingling palm and did her best to ignore her still fluttering nerves. 'Finding the letters. I supposed he's bound to have put them in a safe? We can't hope he would leave them in a drawer?'

Nathan shot her a dry look. 'Would you?'

She winced. 'I don't supposed you can add safe-cracking to your list of accomplishments?' she queried forlornly, and he laughed briefly.

'It wasn't required learning. How about you?' Sighing, she sat back and shrugged. 'I don't get further than opening my cousin's diary with a hairpin. I lost two nails.'

Nathan glanced down at her, eyebrows raised. 'Was it worth it?'

Rachel couldn't help grinning. 'No, it was all pretty tame. She never put in any of the really interesting stuff. And she lied about going out with Rob Maxlow.'

'Who was Rob Maxlow?'

Her lips curled in a reminiscent smile. 'He was captain of the football team. All the girls wanted to date him, but I was the lucky one.'

'Sounds like you started your career at a young age,' Nathan remarked, and she shook her head in vexation.

'God, but you're like a dog with a bone,' she said accusingly. 'For your information I was thirteen years old, and it was all entirely innocent. It may surprise you to know it, but I didn't spring from the womb a fully fledged bitch.'

'I never really thought you did,' Nathan responded apologetically. 'I guess thinking badly of you has become a habit over the years.'

Rachel uttered a wry laugh. 'I had noticed.'

'I suppose you were young and innocent once.

Then you grew up and discovered your power over men and you haven't looked back since.'

She raised an eyebrow at him. 'Are you including yourself in that? Are you admitting I have power over you? she challenged.

He smiled. 'I should have said power over men who don't know you as well as I do,' he corrected smoothly, and Rachel sighed.

'We'll never get beyond my lurid past, will we?' she joked, but deep inside it hurt to know it was no joke. His beliefs were unshakable.

'I cannot take responsibility for your reputation. You made that yourself,' he went on smoothly, and she shook her head in disbelief.

'You're incredible. I've told you before: there could be a perfectly innocent explanation for my behaviour.'

Nathan's response was to rise to his feet and look down at her mockingly. 'I don't think so, sweetheart. Now, I don't know about you, but I'm just about out on my feet. I suggest we go to bed.'

That was too good to miss, and Rachel's lips curved into a flirtatious smile. 'Why, Nathan, that's about the best offer I've had all day!' she quipped, rising to join him.

'Somebody should have paddled your backside a bit more when you were little and it would have done you some good,' he drawled, urging her before him with a hand on the small of her back.

Rachel felt that touch in every part of her, and in instant reaction the tiny hairs on her flesh stood to attention. 'You mean we aren't going to bed after all?' she taunted as they reached the lobby once more.

'Behave yourself, sweetheart, or you might get more than you bargained for,' Nathan promised, reaching round her to press the button for the lift.

'Spoilsport,' she complained, and hastily stifled a yawn as exhaustion and jet lag, despite her afternoon nap, suddenly threatened to sweep over her.

They reached their floor and Nathan let them into their suite. Placing his hands on her shoulders, he turned her towards her bedroom and gave her a small push.

'Go to bed, Rachel.'

She turned with her hand on the doorknob. 'Sure you won't come with me?' The seductive question was spoiled by an even wider yawn this time.

Nathan laughed. 'Even if I were tempted, you're out on your feet.'

He was right, of course, she didn't mean it anyway—well, not much. Which only went to prove just how tired she was. Sighing, she went into the bedroom and closed the door. The bed looked awfully inviting, but from somewhere she found the energy to undress, wash and slip into her nightie before she climbed into it.

The mattress welcomed her like an old friend. It had been an eventful day, and she fully intended running over what she had discovered in her mind, but no sooner had her head hit the pillow than she was asleep.

The car Nathan hired next morning was a showy sports job that shouted of money to burn. They headed north on Route 89, which gave them stunning views of the lake, forests and mountains. Rounding the northern end of Lake Tahoe, they crossed over the state line again and passed through the outdoorsy town of Crystal Bay. From there they followed Ames's directions. As he had said, his house was extremely secluded. Surrounded by trees, and with an unmarked track, without directions they wouldn't have known it was there.

'I don't see any signs of security,' Nathan remarked as he manoeuvred the car along the twisty track. 'No doubt he feels safe out here. Let's hope the house is the same.'

The remark gave her pause for thought. 'What could he have?'

'Infra-red beams. Motion detectors. Heat detectors. Any one of a hundred things.'

'I'm all for security, but that would make it more like a fortress than a home!' she declared with a grimace.

They rounded another bend, and Nathan brought the car to a halt.

'Good heavens!' Rachel exclaimed in surprise. The large two-storey building looked out of keeping with its surroundings. It was as if someone had plucked a small Hollywood mansion from the ground and dropped it here, without thought as to how it would look. 'The man has no taste at all. It even has a tower. I can just see him sitting at the top of it, gloating and drooling over his ill-gotten gains.'

'He certainly makes me feel less critical of my relatives,' Nathan remarked humorously. 'Cousin Edward, our particular black sheep, seems more grey to me now.'

Rachel nodded agreement. 'He's a snake all right. Treating an old woman that way, and a relative to boot! Even my father didn't do that, and he was a first-class rat fink.'

He glanced at her curiously. 'Your parents are divorced, aren't they?'

It was one of the few personal questions he had ever asked her, and her face set in grim lines, as it always did when her father was mentioned. 'Not before time. He's dead now, and I can't say I'm sorry. He never knew how to be faithful, and treated my mother very badly, you know. I don't want to get into that. It all happened a long time ago. I prefer not to think about it.'

'Doesn't sound like you've forgotten it, though.'

She looked at him somberly. 'I learnt a lot of things from my parents' marriage that I never intend to forget. I won't make the same mistakes.'

'It doesn't sound like you had a very happy childhood.'

Rachel shrugged diffidently. It wasn't a subject she cared to talk about too much. 'It wasn't so bad. The bonus was I always had my grandparents to run to when things got too awful. They were marvelous. I discovered through them that there was more to family life than loud voices, crying and slamming doors.'

'You were fortunate,' Nathan said sympathetically. 'Some kids don't have that kind of safety net. What happened to your mother?'

That brought a smile back to Rachel's face. 'She married a really nice man this time. He's an oncologist. They live in Yorkshire. It's good to see her happy at last.'

'Doesn't sound like her experiences put her off marriage,' Nathan observed, but Rachel shook her head.

'Oh, they did, for a long time. She was very cautious. Harry had to work very hard to convince her that marriage to him was the right thing. He won her over, thank goodness.'

'You see a lot of them?'

'As much as I can. It isn't easy, especially now, with my grandparents needing my help. I'm planning to surprise them with an anniversary meal next month,' she revealed, making his brows shoot up.

'You cook, then?'

Rachel sent him a chiding look. 'I run a catering business, remember. What did you think we did? Use magic? I happen to be cordon bleu-trained.'

Blue eyes danced as he returned her look. 'Very impressive. And you partner? Does she cook, too?'

'Of course, though Emma is more of a whiz with pastry than I am. She can invent things that send the calorie count off the scale. You should try some.'

'Perhaps I'll get you to cater one of the bank's functions,' he suggested.

She looked at him suspiciously. 'Ah, but would you trust me with so many wealthy men?'

His mouth curved humorously. 'I doubt you can

be faulted in your professional behaviour. It's up to you, of course, but the offer stands.'

'We could certainly do with all the business we can get. Give me a ring when we get back from this and we'll sort something out,' she agreed.

'Fair enough. OK, let's go join this party,' he said without any enthusiasm, and Rachel laughed.

'I thought you were flattered to be asked to such an…exclusive residence?' she teased him, and he grinned back at her wryly.

'Oh, I am. Can't you tell?' he returned dryly, and Rachel giggled. Nathan's eyes scanned the delight on her face and something flickered briefly in his eyes and was gone in a flash. 'You know, you have a lovely smile,' he said seriously, surprising her so much she blinked at him owlishly.

'I do?' she said faintly, overcome by the unexpected compliment. She hadn't expected him to be so honest.

'Don't sound so surprised,' he drawled as he set the car in motion again.

'But I am. I didn't know there was anything about me you liked.'

He brought the car to a halt near the other halfdozen cars already parked haphazardly outside. He glanced at her broodingly. 'When you smile and laugh, I see the person you could be, rather than the person you are.'

Rachel would dearly have liked to respond to that, but at that moment her door was opened and she glanced round to find a smiling young oriental man waiting for her to alight. As they climbed out, they could hear music and laughter in the distance.

'Good morning, sir. Good morning, miss. Mr Luther said for you to go round to the pool when you arrived. Just follow the path to the left,' the young man directed them.

'Why would a man with a house on the shore have a pool?' she asked out of the side of her mouth.

'I haven't the foggiest idea. I just hope you brought a costume with you,' Nathan remarked as they made their way round the side of the house. 'It looks like we're expected to join in.'

She had. Emma had tucked one in her case at the last minute. But to call it a swimming costume was stretching the point very thin. It wasn't that she disliked wearing skimpy swimwear, but the thought of Luther Ames's eyes wandering over her made her feel very uncomfortable.

They passed through a gap in the shrubbery, and there at the foot of some steps lay a large kidney-shaped pool. There were maybe a half-dozen guests dotted in or around the pool, and Rachel could make out Luther Ames stretched out on a lounger topping up his tan.

'Everyone seems to be having fun,' she said dryly, watching a bronzed young man tossing a buxom brunette into the water.

'How the other half live,' Nathan added, equally dryly, and she gave him a long look.

'Just a minute, we are the other half, remember, and we don't live like this. He has to be the third half.'

Draping an arm around her shoulder, which pulled her in to his side, he started down the steps. 'With maths like that, I'm surprised your business flourishes at all. Did nobody ever throw you into a pool?'

'Not if they wanted to live,' she returned, with a laugh that wobbled faintly. It felt right being this close to Nathan. She could feel every movement of his body, could breathe the scent she always called pure essence of Nathan. It made her want to slip her own arm around his waist, and instantly she realised that she could. The part she was playing would cover her. Heart thumping a little louder, she did that very thing, and her blood pressure rose as their thighs brushed as they walked. It was a heady experience, and one she would remember always. A tiny piece of heaven plucked from a crazy world.

They had been seen by this time, and Luther Ames waved a welcoming hand. 'Come and join us!' he called out, and that moment of intimacy was gone for good. 'Glad you could make it,' he said, shaking hands with Nathan before turning a roving eye on Rachel. 'Sit yourself down right here beside me, Rachel,' he ordered, indicating the empty lounger pulled up close to his.

She didn't want to leave the warmth of Nathan's casual embrace, but that wasn't what she was here for, so, with a silent sigh, she made herself comfortable as requested. 'You have a wonderful house, Mr. Ames,' she flattered, with a sultry smile, going into her act again. 'I've always wanted to sleep in a tower. Do say you've given me a room there!'

Reaching across the tiny gap between them, he took her hand. 'Call me Luther, angel. Sorry, but the tower houses my private rooms. I've put you and Nathan in a room that looks out over the lake.'

Rachel's initial pleasure at learning so easily where Ames's rooms were was spoiled by the knowledge that she and Nathan were sharing a room. Something she realised she should have thought of before. She doubted very much if it was a two—bedded variety, but that was something she would have to deal with later.

She made a small moue of disappointment, then shrugged. 'Oh, well, never mind. Nathan just adores lakes and fishing—don't you, darling?' She appealed to him by kissing her fingers and waggling them in his direction.

Nathan had taken a chair at the near by table and thankfully followed her lead. 'Do you do much fishing, Luther?'

Ames shook his head with a shudder. 'I leave that to the yokels. No, I prefer to sit here and soak up the sun.'

Rachel ran her eyes over the proof of that statement. Ames was a fit man for his age, but there were signs of thickening about his waist. Nevertheless, she cast him a look from beneath her lashes. 'I just love a man with a tan,' she flirted, and Ames grinned back at her suggestively.

'Then this must be my lucky day. I love a woman who loves men with tans. Especially if she's blonde and very, very beautiful.'

She gave a tiny feline stretch, as if to make herself

more comfortable. 'Mmm...I think I'm going to like it here.'

Ames turned on his side, propping his head on his arm the better to see her. 'You must let me show you over the house...unless Nathan would object?' He took his gaze off her long enough to look at the other man. However, it was Rachel who answered.

'Oh, Nathan won't mind, will you, darling?' she declared, casting him a glance, then did a swift double-take. Nathan was frowning at her, and her heart skidded as she wondered what she had done wrong. Then it struck her that of course he would frown if he felt she was being poached from him. It was all part of the act. To which end she uttered a tinkling laugh. 'He gets a little jealous, you know. I'm his lucky mascot, you see. He doesn't want to lose me.'

'Neither would I, if you were mine,' Ames responded huskily, stroking her arm lightly.

She didn't like the possessive way he did it, and quickly placed a hand over his to stop him. 'You wouldn't really try and steal me away, now, would you?' she asked archly, and he grinned.

'Could I?' he countered, and she sighed.

'We-ell, a girl ought to keep her options open, don't you think?'

Ames laughed. 'I do indeed. Angel, I think you and I are going to get along very well.'

Nathan had said very little whilst all this side-play was going on, but Rachel was very much aware of him. The vibrations he was giving off made her want to shiver. If she hadn't known it was all an act...but she did, so there was no point speculating otherwise.

Now he rose and came across, reaching out a hand to her.

'Come along, darling, let's find our room and change into something less formal,' he suggested coolly, and with an apologetic smile in Ames's direction she took his hand and allowed him to pull her to her feet.

Ames sat up, a mocking look in his eye. 'Hope I'm not treading on your toes, Nathan. I just like to keep the ladies amused.'

Nathan smiled back with concealed insincerity. 'Rachel's a free agent. I never tie her down because I know she'll always come back to me.'

Ames didn't look quite so amused now, and waved a hand at a servant who had been hovering, awaiting orders. 'Have Michael show my friends here to their room. Lunch will be served on the terrace in half an hour. We'll meet again then.' Turning away, he dived neatly into the pool and began doing laps.

Rachel glanced at Nathan, but his expression was as smooth as glass. She had no idea what he was thinking. She found out, though, the instant the silent efficient Michael had shown them to their room.

The door closed softly, and Nathan turned to her with a grim look on his face. 'Just what the devil do you think you're playing at?' he demanded furiously.

CHAPTER SIX

RACHEL'S lips parted on a gasp of surprise. 'Excuse me?'

A nerve ticked in Nathan's jaw. 'Don't play dumb. I'm referring to the game you were playing with Ames out by the pool!' he enlarged grittily.

She simply couldn't believe she was actually hearing this. Amazed at this totally unexpected attack, she took umbrage. Eyes narrowing dangerously, she crossed her arms aggressively. 'I was doing what *you* asked me to do!' she countered, with what she considered justifiable indignation. The man had said flirt with Ames, and that was precisely what she had done. No more, no less. What could he find wrong in that?

Apparently quite a lot. Some deep emotion flashed ominously in his eyes. 'That didn't mean you had to crawl all over him like a rash!' he thundered back through clenched teeth.

Her chin went up at that crack. Well, of all the nerve! She had done nothing of the sort. 'I wasn't all over him. I...'

The angry words tailed off abruptly as she suddenly fell into what was happening here. It was staggering. What she had thought downstairs had been part of the act was, in actual fact, very real. He was furious with her for doing what was expected of her.

Her heart took a crazy lurch, for she could think of only one reason for his behaviour. A reason which took her breath away whilst it opened up a realm of possibilities. Yet she responded to it with caution, in case she was misreading the signs, protecting herself by acting in character.

'Why, Nathan, I do believe you're jealous!' she exclaimed gleefully, and all the while her heart was tripping crazily in her chest at the thought of what could be possible.

Immediately a shutter went down over those scintillating blue eyes. 'Now that is the most ridiculous thing I've ever heard you say!'

Hearing such an emphatic denial, the more certain was she that she was right. He *was* jealous. Taking great care, she spread her hands in a sign of mystification. 'Then why are you so angry?'

'I am not angry!' he denied, so forcefully that for the life of her she couldn't help laughing.

'Of course not!' she agreed, smiling broadly, eyes dancing.

He was far from amused already, and that, apparently, was a step too far. He closed the distance between them in one swift stride, voice dropping warningly. 'Don't laugh at me, Rachel,' he advised softly.

She tried, but the knowledge she had just gained acted on her like fine wine. She was drunk on it, and a giggle escaped her. 'I can't help it. You're so funny!'

'I'm warning you. Stop it, or I'll stop you!' he threatened, and Rachel went still, her eyes locking with his. Suddenly the air was positively seething with suppressed emotions, making it hard to breathe.

'And just how do you propose to do that?' she taunted softly, thinking she had to be crazy to be baiting this man, but too caught up to stop now. So much was at stake, it was time to be reckless.

That dangerous something flashed in his eyes again the second before he caught her by the upper arms and yanked her to him. 'Like this!' he growled, and brought his mouth down on hers.

It was everything Rachel had dreamt it would be, and a whole lot more. She had never believed it would happen, and now that it had she quite forgot to breathe. At first Nathan's lips were hard on hers, revealing his anger, but he couldn't maintain it, and within seconds the pressure altered subtly, taking on an urgency that sought a response from her that she was only too happy to give. This was no gentle seduction, but she didn't care. Her lips parted, welcoming the thrust of his tongue, meeting it with her own. Like two combustible chemicals, they came together and became an explosive mixture. His hands released their hold as his arms slid around her, pulling her crushingly close. It was as if he could not get enough of her, and, quivering with newly awakened desire, she knew that she wanted more too.

From nowhere, this sexual conflagration swept over them with the effect of a forest fire. They were hungry for each other, and the air positively sizzled with the force of this sudden need. Her whole body trembled, her nerve-endings so receptive she was almost humming with the incredible pleasure of his lips on hers and the feel of his body hard against her own. Even then the need was to get closer, and when one powerful thigh thrust between hers she went up in flames with a helpless moan.

Perversely, it was that small sound which brought Nathan back to his senses. He tore his mouth from hers and, breathing heavily, stared down at her incredulously.

Rachel looked up at him dreamily, her eyes half-closed, her lips bruised by the power of his kisses. 'Oh, Nathan, don't stop...' she sighed, attempting to put her arms around his neck and pull his head back down to hers, but that was too much. He thrust her away from him and she staggered backwards, only regaining her balance with an effort.

Nathan dragged a visibly trembling hand through his hair and glared at her. 'Damn it, I knew you'd try something like this!' he accused, stunning her in quite a different way.

Even so, it didn't take her addled brain long to realise that he was placing the blame on her. Whilst she would have been prepared to share it, she had no intention of taking it all on herself. 'Hey, just a second. *You* kissed *me*, remember!' she countered swiftly, coming out of her kiss induced daze with a vengeance.

He shot her an icy look. 'You had nothing to do with it, of course!'

Rachel shook her head in sheer disbelief. 'I didn't make you do anything you didn't want to do!' He could have broken off the kiss when it had still been a punishment, but he had chosen to prolong it and the kiss had changed dramatically. What was sticking in his craw was the fact he hadn't been able to help himself any more than she had.

He rounded on her with a look that would have made lesser mortals back off, but Rachel was made of sterner stuff and stood her ground, albeit with a thudding heart. 'Do you imagine for one second that I really wanted to kiss you?'

That hurt, because he knew as well as she did who had been in control. She jerked her chin at him belligerently. 'It certainly felt like it to me!'

That nerve started up in his jaw again. 'Take it from me, you were wrong.'

'Liar,' she accused, the word slipping out before she could consider the consequences of saying it.

Nathan looked as if he wanted to resort to violence. 'Nobody gets away with calling me a liar,' he declared with dire promise, and though Rachel's heart skipped a vital beat she stayed where she was.

'What are you going to do, kiss me again?' she taunted, whilst part of her longed for that very thing. She was hooked. One kiss would never be enough.

A nasty smile twisted his handsome mouth. 'You'd like that, wouldn't you?'

Unable to back down, and knowing the real Rachel would show too much hurt at the way he was destroying a moment she had felt was so precious, she hid once again behind the person he thought her to be.

'I wouldn't say no. That kiss certainly had potential. It's a shame you ended it so soon,' she complained with a touch of mockery.

His chest expanded as he drew in a deep, steadying breath. Lowering his head, he placed his hands on his hips and studied the tips of his shoes for a long moment before glancing up at her again. She could see immediately that his anger had been mastered, and there was only a glittering mockery in his eyes.

'Don't play games with me, Rachel. I warned you about that before.'

It seemed to Rachel that they had come a long way in the last few minutes and were still nowhere. She couldn't let it go without hitting back. 'At least admit that you enjoyed kissing me,' she goaded, slinking towards him with her head tipped on one side consideringly. 'Or aren't you man enough to do that?'

'Oh, I enjoyed kissing you,' he admitted without hesitation, and the irony in his eyes was painful to witness. 'That doesn't mean I'd want to do it again. After all, I like sugar, but I avoid it because I know it's bad for me.'

She pouted prettily, whilst inside she knew she could be good for him if he would only give her the chance to prove it. 'That must take a lot of the fun out of your life.'

He smiled thinly, 'I know, but at least I'll live longer. Now, I suggest you shift that delightful backside of yours into gear and get ready for lunch, before they send out a search party.'

Saving face being the priority, Rachel picked up

her case and headed for the bathroom, pausing briefly in the doorway to give him a sly look. 'How interesting. You like kissing me. You like my back-side. You even think I have a lovely smile. I'd be careful, Nathan, darling, for these are worrying signs. Who knows where it will end?' she taunted, and closed the door on any possible answer he cared to make.

The energy went out of her in a rush then. She sagged back against the door and closed her eyes. Automatically her hand rose to her mouth, her fingers probing lips which still tingled. So much had happened she scarcely knew where to begin, but the main thing she would never forget was how Nathan had kissed her. He had been angry to start with, but desire had quickly over-mastered it. For a few vital moments he had dropped his guard and given himself up to her. Of course, after that it had all gone wrong, yet there was no ignoring the revelation of his anger. He hadn't liked her flirting with Ames, despite the fact that that was what she had been brought here to do.

A smile slowly curved her lips. She knew when a man wanted her, and Nathan had certainly wanted her just now. He was jealous because he wanted her. He had given himself away unmistakably, and he knew it. That was why he was fighting such a dirty rearguard action. But it was too late. His defences had been compromised. He should never have been angry. That had been his first mistake. His second had been telling her he didn't want to kiss her again, when he had kissed her in a way that said the opposite. Once wouldn't be enough, not now he knew what he was missing.

She shook her head in wonder. All this time he had been hiding his attraction to her, just as she had been hiding hers to him. After all his protestations to the contrary, he was not immune to her, and never had been. She had discovered the chink in his armour. He used words to keep her at a distance, because the minute he touched her he went up in flames.

With a sigh she pushed herself away from the door and set her case on the toilet seat. OK, she knew that wanting wasn't love, but it was a start. The smile faded as she considered where they went from here. One thing was certain: he wouldn't come to her; she would have to do the seducing. It would be no easy job to undermine his resistance, and if he should smother his dislike of who he thought she was enough to want an affair with her would she want that? Her body might, but her heart was another matter.

But that was putting the cart before the horse. For now it was enough to know that he was powerfully attracted to her. That was where she had to start her campaign if she wanted to win their private war. There would be time enough later to decide just how far she wanted to go.

All through lunch Rachel kept up a light flirtation with Ames, who was all too ready to join in the game. What Nathan thought of her behaviour she had no means of knowing, for though he laughed and joked, and made light conversation with the other members of the party, there was a shutter down over his eyes which gave nothing away.

It irked her no end, and caused her to flirt more outrageously, which got her nowhere except in possible deep water with Ames who, not knowing what she was about, took it seriously. She had changed into a pair of very short shorts and a skimpy top which defied gravity only by means of two pencil-thin straps. Nathan, having settled on trousers and a short-sleeved shirt, had taken one look at her and his jaw had set disapprovingly, yet he said nothing. Ames couldn't keep his eyes off her, and had rained compliments on her constantly. When, after lunch, he suggested once again that he show her over the house, the hairs stood up on the back of her neck in alarm. Automatically she turned to Nathan.

'Honey, Luther's going to show me round the house. Do you want to join us?' she invited lightly, but her eyes sent a message that she expected him to say yes. Fortunately for her, Ames was the kind of man who liked to show off his possessions, and consequently added his invitation to hers.

'Please do. I have a large collection of antique jade and ivory which may interest you,' he said, in that offhand way which implied he expected his guests to be suitably impressed.

Much to her relief, Nathan inclined his head in agreement. 'I have a small collection of netsuke and inro myself,' he remarked modestly, and Ames smiled in faint interest, for he much preferred to be the centre of attention.

Standing, he helped Rachel to her feet and tucked her hand in his arm possessively. 'Really? Then you must give me your verdict on my humble display. This way.' He led the way into the house. Nathan smiled faintly, tucked his hands in the pockets of his trousers and ambled after them.

'Wouldn't your other guests like to come, too?' Rachel enquired, but Ames merely laughed.

'Oh, they've seen it many times before. We'll leave them to amuse themselves for a while.'

Ames's 'humble' collection was displayed in cases throughout the house. He had eclectic tastes, but expensive ones. Rachel had lived with antique porcelain and china all her life, and recognised good pieces when she saw them. Not that she said so.

'How much did you say you paid for this?' she asked of a Meissen figurine she held.

Ames shrugged. 'Oh, I believe it was a mere snip at $30,000,' he said idly. 'There are only two in the world.'

She raised her eyebrows expressively. 'You paid that for this?' she exclaimed, in tones which said he had to be crazy, though she had always thought it a wonderful piece. Her grandmother had owned the pair to it, and had left it to Rachel in her will.

Ames didn't seem at all surprised that she was less than impressed. It was what he expected of her. 'You have to have an eye to appreciate it,' he declared, retrieving the piece and restoring it to the display case.

Rachel shrugged. 'I guess that's so. I was just

thinking of all the clothes I could have bought with that kind of money.' She sighed wistfully.

'That's a hint to me that she still wants to go shopping,' Nathan observed dryly, and Rachel turned an offended shoulder and puffed up her hair.

'A promise is a promise, I say. You wouldn't go back on a promise, would you, Luther?' she charged, batting her eyes at him and giving Nathan a frosty look.

Ames appeared to enjoy the by-play, and she knew it would give him great pleasure to split them up. He was the sort of man who enjoyed such pettiness. It was to their good that they could use it against him.

'I would never go back on a promise I made to *you*, angel,' he declared fulsomely, and, preening, Rachel slipped her arm through his and brushed herself up against him.

'Now that's what I like to hear,' she said huskily, and thought she caught the faintest hint of a muffled growl issuing from Nathan's throat.

'What was that, darling?' she asked limpidly, glancing over her shoulder at him, her breath hitching when she caught sight of that telltale tic in his jaw. As a barometer of his displeasure it was registering stormy weather ahead, and boosted her morale instantly.

'Just clearing my throat,' he responded, with a flash of fire at the back of his eyes, and a tiny feline smile curved her lips at this further sign of displeasure. By doing wrong she was doing something right!

'You said something about ivory?' Nathan diverted the conversation abruptly, and Ames shot him a faintly mocking look.

'So I did,' he conceded. 'It's this way.'

He took them up to his own private rooms in the tower and threw open the door. 'Now, tell me what you think of that,' he said proudly.

Rachel had never seen so much ivory and jade in one place, but, though she admired the jade, no matter how old the ivory was she couldn't forget the elephants which had been killed to provide it. Nathan was taking a much closer look, and Ames watched him with barely concealed excitement.

'You have some very fine pieces here,' Nathan remarked after he had toured the cases and started round again.

'A netsuke came on the market several months ago. It would have made the collection complete. Unfortunately it went for a small fortune to a mystery buyer,' Ames remarked with annoyance.

Nathan glanced at him with a faint smile. 'Yes. I considered it money well spent,' he said casually, stunning Ames out of his puffed-up pride.

'*You* were the mystery buyer?' he ejaculated incredulously.

'It now has pride of place in my collection,' Nathan confirmed. 'Rachel thinks I should have spent the money on her,' he added sardonically, quirking an eyebrow in her direction.

Feeling all at sea, she somehow managed to respond. 'It's such a little thing, and nobody ever sees it except you, darling. I can't see what you see in it!' she said grumpily.

'Of course you can't!' Ames declared irritably, and if she hadn't been playing a role she might have been offended. As it was, she barely caught back a startled giggle. 'You can't see beyond the glitter of diamonds, but Nathan and I can.'

'Well!' she exclaimed, pretending to be affronted. 'I don't think that's very nice!' But she went ignored. Ames had bigger fish to fry.

'How much do you want for it?' he asked Nathan bluntly, who showed only mild surprise at his host's tone.

'I have no intention of selling. As I said, it's the pride of my collection.'

Ames made a valiant attempt to curb his frustration, but he was clearly not the most patient of men. 'You must at least let me try to persuade you. I simply won't take no for an answer,' he said, trying to make light of it.

Nathan laughed. 'I can't stop you trying, but it's only fair to warn you I'm a hard nut to crack.'

Ames laughed too. 'There would be no fun if you weren't. Now, I think we've abandoned the others long enough, don't you?' He indicated they should move to the door, but as they did so the telephone rang on the desk. 'Do excuse me. I must answer that,' he apologised.

Nathan slid an arm around Rachel's waist and herded her out ahead of him. 'No problem. We can find our way back,' he said calmly, and closed the door behind them.

They walked down the passageway that led back

to the main staircase, and it was a little while before Rachel realised Nathan was laughing.

'What on earth is so funny?' she asked, smiling herself at his patent amusement but mystified as to its cause.

'Ames, of course,' he replied, scarcely shedding any light.

'I fail to see what's so amusing about telling someone we know to be a thief that you have a priceless antique that he covets beyond anything else. I hope your home is alarmed, because if you don't sell to him he'll probably arrange to steal it!' she exclaimed in some concern, but that only made him smile more broadly.

'He'd have a job,' Nathan responded dryly, and suddenly she saw the light.

'You don't have it, do you?' she charged in admiration.

'Nope,' he confirmed, grinning.

She shook her head at his nerve. 'I believed you!'

'So did Ames, and that is far more important. If all else fails, we now have a bargaining chip.'

'Very clever. But you don't have the ivory to swap,' she pointed out dryly.

'Ah, but Ames doesn't know that. A good poker player has to know when to bluff.'

She stared at him in wonder. 'Lord, but you frighten me sometimes. I can't read you at all.'

'Good. Let's hope Ames suffers from the same failing, hmm?' Nathan rejoined as they descended to the entrance hall. Rachel added a silent amen to that.

'Not that I approve of you having an ivory collection at all,' she reproved him, wanting to make her position clear. 'It's people like you and Ames who keep the disgusting trade alive. If people didn't buy ivory, poachers would be out of a job and valuable animals would still be alive.'

Nathan studied her animated face in amusement. 'I agree with you one hundred per cent.'

The wind having been taken out of her sails, she looked at him suspiciously. 'You do?'

He nodded seriously, though his eyes glinted with humour. 'Absolutely. If you want the truth, I don't collect ivory, in any shape or form. I simply used it as a ploy to get into Ames's private rooms. Now we know exactly where they are, it will be easier to search them.'

Rachel listened to his explanation in exasperation. She had read him the Riot Act quite unnecessarily. 'You might have told me,' she complained.

'There wasn't time,' Nathan pointed out, and she reluctantly admitted that was true. They were having to think on their feet, and so far each had been quick enough to back the other up. She just hoped they could keep it up.

She glanced at the archway which would take them to the patio and the other guests, and pulled a face. 'I suppose we do have to join them?' she asked without enthusiasm.

Nathan took a quick look round, then caught her arm and steered her in the opposite direction. 'Not if we can avoid it. Let's go down to the lake. At least there we can be sure of some privacy. We need to talk, and I get the uneasy feeling these walls have ears.'

CHAPTER SEVEN

BY DINT of testing doors as they went, they eventually found a side entrance and made good their escape. They must look like a couple of schoolkids dodging lessons, she thought with a smothered giggle. To their left there was a somewhat overgrown path through the undergrowth bounding the house, and without hesitation they followed it as it appeared to be heading off in the right direction.

'What if Luther misses us?' Rachel queried, stepping over a rotting log that had almost tripped her up.

'That's easy. You gave us the perfect excuse earlier. As a keen angler, where else would I go but down to the lake?' he replied dryly, and she spared him a glance, for something had just that moment occurred to her.

'Er…as a matter of interest, do you fish?' she asked tentatively.

'Now she asks me!' Nathan exclaimed with a groan. 'Don't worry. I doubt very much if I'll be asked to prove my prowess in that direction.'

'I didn't mean to drop you in it like that. It just seemed a good idea,' Rachel apologised, pushing aside an overhanging branch. 'Grandfather will tell you I have this tendency to jump in without thinking, and I assumed as a man you could fish.'

Nathan barely prevented the branch from hitting him in the face as she released it. 'Oh, I can fish all right. Whenever the opportunity arises, I head up to the Scotland for some fly fishing.'

'Really? I'm surprised you find the time, what with your women and all!' she couldn't resist retorting mockingly. 'Or do you take them with you for light relief when the fish aren't biting?'

'You know, that tongue of yours is going to get you into all sorts of trouble,' Nathan warned silkily.

'Promises, promises,' she jibed, just as they burst out of the undergrowth onto the lakeshore. Words dried on her tongue at the scene which opened up before them.

The lake stretched out as far as the eye could see. Sun danced on the ripples of water as it broke over the rocks at the water's edge. It was as if they had walked through a portal into a different world. They found themselves in a perfect little cove, where dappled sunlight fell on the grassy banks. All that could be heard was the buzzing of bees and the melodious calls of distant birds.

Rachel was glad now that she had changed into those shorts, for it allowed her to kick off her shoes and wade knee-deep into the water. It was sheer bliss, and she threw back her head, raising her face to the sun.

'You look like some pagan water goddess.' Nathan's voice interrupted her hedonistic pleasure and she glanced round, shading her eyes against the sun's glare.

He was standing watching her with his hands

braced on his hips, and he looked so powerful and sexy her mouth went dry. All at once she wanted him to kiss her quite badly. And, if the heat in his eyes wasn't just a trick of the sun, he was thinking about that kiss they had shared, too. It was time to put on a little pressure, to take the fight to him.

'Why don't you join me?' she invited with a smile, holding out her hand to him.

'Wouldn't that spoil the effect? I can admire your luscious body better from here,' he replied sardonically, and she dropped her hand. Her smile turned sultry, for she knew his tactic of using words against her now.

'Is that what you think I'm doing? Trying to entice you?' she asked, with just the right hint of husky seductiveness.

'It had occurred to me,' he responded dryly. 'I thought it best to tell you you were wasting your time.'

'Oh, I wouldn't say that,' she corrected as she waded to the shore with an exaggerated swing of her hips. 'After all, you got a good look in before feeling compelled to put me straight,' she added with heavy irony. As she brushed past him she reached up and ran her fingers over his jaw caressingly. 'I don't mind you looking at me, Nathan darling. I don't mind at all.'

Smiling to herself, for she had caught the flash of annoyance in his eyes, she went to the nearest sunny patch of grass and flung herself down on it, folding her arms behind her head.

'This isn't going to work, you know,' he told. 'I'm not about to let myself be seduced by you.'

She feigned surprise. 'Am I trying to seduce you?'

'It sounds like it to me,' he retorted, and she laughed softly.

'Well, you should know. You've had enough practice yourself.'

'Precisely, so you know I know all the tricks. Why don't you give up whilst you're ahead, hmm?'

Rachel sent him a knowing look. 'Would you, if you were me?'

Nathan rubbed his thumb along the ridge of his nose, and finally sighed ruefully. 'I guess not. OK, do your worst, if you must, but don't say I didn't warn you.'

Oh, she knew what the danger was better than he. Nathan was thinking solely of her pride, whilst she knew he could break her heart. Still, she was prepared to risk it, for a faint heart never won anything. And if all else failed she could still take refuge in the character he disliked so much. He would never know she loved him.

She patted the ground beside her invitingly. 'The grass is lovely and soft. Why don't you join me? You should learn to relax more, you know.'

'I'll relax when this is over. Right now there isn't time.'

Which, deplore it though she might, was no less than the truth. 'OK, I get the message. This is strictly business. So tell me, what are we going to do now? Do I keep Luther busy whilst you look? Or should

I slip out whilst you're playing cards? Maybe I could get an invite to his bedroom,' she added goadingly, and his head shot round as if it was on a swivel.

'Stay out of his room, Rachel. That's an order!'

There was nothing feigned about his disapproval, and she wondered if he realised how much he was giving away every time he responded so angrily. She came up on her knees and executed a rakish salute. 'Yes, sir!' she snapped out, and was delighted to see his lips twitch. She liked making him laugh, especially when he didn't want to.

'Cut it out, sweetheart. Just remember there are certain things in this crazy enterprise of ours that you aren't required to do,' he told her seriously, and she loved him for saying it. He wouldn't throw her to the wolf, no matter what.

She smiled winningly. 'I'm glad to hear it. There is only one pair of arms I'm interested in having around me.'

Nathan drew in a ragged breath and shot her a long-suffering look. 'Can we keep to the point?'

She immediately folded her hands in her lap obediently, eyeing him attentively. 'OK, I'm listening.'

It was plain Nathan fought with an urge to do something physical, and, to her regret, mastered it. 'It's best if we play this by ear. We don't want to make Ames suspicious. Whichever of us gets the first opportunity should take it. I...'

He said more, but Rachel had stopped listening. She found herself watching his mouth as he talked, remembering the feel of it on hers. Then there were his hands. He used them to underline what he was saying. They were strong and tanned, and she longed to feel them on her skin. So strong was the need that she didn't want to wait. Nor did she have to. Fate took a hand. Somewhere in the woods behind them an unwary animal stepped on a twig and snapped it. When she realised Nathan hadn't heard it, she saw it as an omen and took her chance.

With a faint cry of alarm she flung herself at him, catching his look of surprise just before her lips found his, cutting off what he had been saying. Nathan tumbled backwards, his arms instinctively locking around her as he fell. At the last minute he rolled sideways, taking her beneath him. The kiss was broken, and he frowned down at her in dark suspicion.

'What the devil are you playing at?' he demanded to know, and she shook her head vehemently.

'Shush! Somebody's coming,' she lied in an urgent whisper, and slipped her arms around his neck to drag his head back down to hers.

He resisted, head cocked, listening. 'I don't hear anything,' he responded equally softly.

Rachel groaned inwardly. Trust him to argue. She tugged on his neck, bringing his head a little closer. 'I tell you I heard something!' she insisted, and his eyes locked on hers searchingly. Clearly he didn't know whether to believe her or not. 'Nathan!' she persisted urgently, and at the sound of his name his gaze dropped to her lips, scorching them with his glance, then travelled up to lock with her eyes.

She could see the banked fires in the blue depths

and knew that vital sexual awareness had sparked to life when their bodies had touched. He didn't believe her, but he wanted to kiss her, and the battle he fought was with himself. She knew when it was over, for he gave a guttural groan and closed the gap separating them.

His body came down on hers as he angled his head, the better to kiss her. She welcomed his weight with a tiny sigh of satisfaction, giving herself up to the pleasure of his drugging kisses. Free at last to respond, she allowed her hands to rove over the taut contours of his back, then slid one hand into the lush thickness of his hair and let it curl sinuously around her fingers. It was like silk, and she gloried in the feel of it, losing herself in the moment.

When Nathan's lips left hers and traced a path to her throat, she arched her neck into that burning caress with a tiny moan. His tongue darted out, tasting her, and she shivered. One large hand glided over her hip, skimmed along her ribs and found the mound of her breast. She felt herself swell into the cup of his palm, her aroused nipple pushing upwards in silent demand. He answered it with the sweep of his thumb, causing her to gasp as her stomach clenched on a powerful wave of desire.

She moved beneath him restlessly, feeling the response of his body, knowing his desire was as strong as her own. He rocked his hips against hers and she moved to accommodate him, frustrated that the barrier of their clothes kept them from the closeness she longed for. Then his fingers brushed her skimpy top aside and his mouth closed on her breast and she forgot to think. Her fingers took a death-grip on his hair as his tongue teased her turgid flesh, his teeth grazing the proud peak into a hard nub of pleasure.

Automatically her free hand scrabbled at his shirt, dragging it from his trousers so that finally she could touch him. He was hot and silky and she gloried in the way his body moved in reaction to her soft exploration.

'Oh…yes, Nathan. Yes,' she sighed achingly as his mouth continued its moist caress, and that brought his head up, his eyes gleaming hot and passionate.

'Have they gone yet?' he asked huskily, brushing his lips along her jaw, sending her thoughts haywire.

'Yes. No. I don't know,' she groaned, then felt compelled to confess. 'I lied.'

He looked at her again, whilst his hand traced a path to her thigh and stroked it gently. 'I know.'

One hand slipped under her shorts, finding the curve of her bottom, and her eyelids fluttered. 'I wanted you to kiss me,' she sighed raggedly.

His hand stilled and he stared down at her, jaw clenching, 'I wanted to kiss you, too.' he admitted, and her lips, swollen from his passionate kisses, curved into an encouraging smile.

'That wasn't so difficult to say, was it?' she teased softly. 'Let's try it again,' she suggested, but didn't get the response she expected.

Nathan closed his eyes for a moment, then abruptly pushed himself up, away from her. Turning to face the water, he wrapped his arms around his knees. 'My God, I underestimated you badly,' he declared in a voice loaded with self-disgust.

Realising he was not about to come back to her, Rachel sighed and straightened her clothes. Chilled by his abrupt desertion, she tipped her head so that she had the perfect view of his broad-shouldered torso.

'How? You knew it was a trick all the time,' she charged, in a voice made husky by passion.

'Sure I did, but you were so good I almost forgot what I know about you,' he shot back with another incredulous shake of his head.

Her heart leapt at the confession that, for a time at least, he had forgotten who she was. It had to mean she was making progress. 'I keep telling you there's a lot you don't know about me,' she replied softly.

He rolled his neck, easing out the kinks. 'When it comes to you I know too much already.'

Her lips twisted into a pained grimace, for she knew where he was going. Somehow, no matter where they started, their conversations had a way of turning full circle and coming back to that scene he had witnessed. 'And as far as you're concerned all of it is bad,' she agreed dryly. 'Does it matter so much?'

That brought his head round, their eyes meeting and locking. 'It matters, sweetheart, because it makes it hard for me to like you,' he revealed simply, surprising the breath out of her.

'I didn't know you wanted to like me!' she exclaimed breathlessly, her heart catching in her throat. 'Why would you want to?' she asked, feeling the answer had an importance way beyond the obvious, but not knowing why.

Blue eyes scanned her face, then met her eyes again. After what they had just shared the shutters were absent, allowing her to see the blatant desire he felt for her. 'Why? Because it would make wanting you a hell of a lot easier to accept,' he said bluntly, and her heart stopped, before rushing on madly.

She hadn't expected this confession, but she knew she had to feel her way carefully. 'You finally admit you want me, then?'

A rueful smile twisted his lips as he nodded. 'It would be foolish not to, when I've given myself away so obviously,' he went on. 'I always knew you were trouble with a capital T. You're talented and intelligent. Undeniably beautiful, and sexy as hell. If it wasn't for that damned flaw in your character this conversation would be redundant.'

It was stunning to realise what he meant. But for that one sticking point they wouldn't be wasting time talking now, they would be making love. The prospect set her nerves fluttering in her stomach.

'Couldn't you simply forget about it?' she suggested a little hoarsely, and he shook his head.

'I'd only remember it again.'

Her eyebrows rose fractionally. 'Is that another way of saying you'd hate yourself in the morning?' she quipped faintly, and his lips twitched.

'I guess so. It would be easy for me to lock the facts away whilst I sate myself with your body, but the trouble is I don't use women that way.' He turned away from her again, looking out over the shining water pensively. 'If things were different...' He left the sentence hanging tantalisingly.

Rachel felt her heart kick, and knew she couldn't leave it there. 'Yes? If things were different?' she probed, and he sighed and looked her squarely in the eye, his expression uncompromising.

'But they're not different, Rachel. I know what I know. You are who you are.'

Except she wasn't who he thought. But how did she go about convincing him? Emma was right. She had dug herself a hole that was now almost too big to climb out of. Still, she had to try, for she could feel herself this close to something incredibly valuable. Reaching out, she laid her hand on his back. It was warm to the touch and sent tingles up her arm.

'Sometimes things aren't what they seem, Nathan,' she began softly, and a rueful expression crossed his face.

'And sometimes that's all they are.'

She frowned at the interruption. 'Yes, but there are things you don't know. I...' He stopped her with a finger pressed to her lips.

'Don't. I don't want to know anything else.'

Rachel caught his wrist and pushed his hand away. 'You have to listen. I haven't been honest with you!' she insisted, determined to tell him the truth about what he had seen that summer so long ago.

'If we're talking about honesty, I haven't been

honest either. Earlier you accused me of being jealous, and you were right. I've wanted you for a very long time,' he admitted coolly, completely distracting her from what she needed to say.

'Really? You hid it very well,' she couldn't help retorting dryly, and that made him smile.

'Did I? Sometimes I thought I was being glaringly obvious. In all honesty I want you so badly right now it's hard to keep my hands off you. However, the fact is I gain no pleasure from wanting you. I have to respect the woman I have a relationship with,' he continued softly. 'That's why there can never be anything between us.'

She had always known how he felt, but hearing it was still a blow, and she couldn't let it pass. Green eyes held blue, and, taking a deep breath, she made yet another attempt to tell him the truth. 'Nathan, about what you thought you saw—'

Interrupting her, Nathan traced his knuckles along the fragile line of her jaw with unexpected tenderness. 'I *know* what I saw, Rachel. There's nothing you can say to make me change my mind about you. I'm just a toy to you, sweetheart. Something you want because you can't have it. However much I might want to take you to bed, I won't use or be used by you just to satisfy a sexual urge.'

She could have told him differently, but she knew he wouldn't believe her. Just as she knew he wouldn't believe the truth she had just tried to tell him. He would never love her because of her 'past'. She had to cut her losses. All she was ever likely to share with him was a passionate affair, and even that would take some doing—if she really wanted it.

She hid her regret behind a jaunty smile. 'Are you sure that's all it is? A sexual urge?'

His eyes roved her body, starting flash fires on her skin. 'Oh, yes. A pretty powerful one,' he admitted gruffly.

That at least gave her hope. He wanted her, and at least an affair, however brief it might be, would give her something to remember in the long days and nights ahead. She had to go for it.

'Are you sure I can't persuade you to change your mind and go with the flow?' she teased seductively, and not surprisingly he shook his head.

'Just write me up in your diary as the one that got away,' he refused lightly, and her heart cried out. For he was the only one she wanted, and she now knew that, but for that scene he had witnessed, they could have shared something wonderful.

It was a bitter fact to accept that she had played her part so well he would never believe her, but she had no choice. All she could do was swallow the lump of emotion blocking her throat and laugh huskily. 'Damn you, Nathan Wade, but you're a hard man to seduce!' she exclaimed sardonically, sitting up and resting her chin on her knees, needing to keep her too expressive face from his scrutiny lest she give her true feelings away.

'I'm glad to see you're taking it so well,' Nathan remarked humorously, and she had mastered her emotions enough to shoot him an old-fashioned look.

'Surely you didn't expect me to throw myself in the lake over you?' she countered mockingly.

'Nothing so dramatic,' he returned with a shrug. 'I guess I expected tears at the very least. You constantly surprise me.'

No kidding! Rachel thought, then said airily, 'Perhaps that's because I'm no ordinary woman.'

He laughed softly. 'Without a doubt, ordinary is something you will never be. You've got style, anyway.'

'Just not enough of it, apparently,' she retorted wryly, then something occurred to her and she looked at him curiously. 'Tell me something, Nathan. If you want me as badly as you say you do, why don't you try to change me?' she ventured challengingly, and he stared at her thoughtfully.

'It might be interesting to try,' he admitted eventually.

She was by instinct a fighter, and he was so adamant that there would be nothing between them that it virtually compelled her to do all she could to seduce him, even knowing she was the one who would end up being hurt. Notwithstanding that she glanced at him sideways. 'What's stopping you?'

'I doubt you'd want to change.'

Her half-smile was pure provocation. 'Perhaps not. On the other hand, you might find you don't want me to change. After all, we're only talking about an affair here. A little danger would spice things up.'

He laughed, but there was a light in his eye that

set her nerves leaping. 'When you put it like that, it would almost be worth it.'

'What have you got to lose? It would be good, Nathan. You know it would,' she enticed in a husky undertone.

'Maybe.'

With a shake of her head, she clambered to her feet. 'I haven't given up, you know. By hook or by crook, we *will* end up in bed together.'

That had him lifting an eyebrow as he rose to join her. 'Somewhere along the line our roles have been reversed. Isn't that what I should be saying to you?'

Rachel grinned flirtatiously back at him. 'Exactly. The difference is, *I* wouldn't be saying no.'

This time it was Nathan who shook his head. 'You've got more nerve than any woman I know.'

She shrugged. 'When I know what I want, I go after it.'

'And if what you want doesn't want you?' he countered smoothly, at which she smiled seductively.

'But you do want me, Nathan. You've just said so. And even if you hadn't, your body said it for you. You just won't take a chance. What harm can an affair with me possibly do you?'

Those magnificent blue eyes looked at her consideringly. 'Perhaps you should be asking yourself that question,' he suggested silkily.

Crossing to him, she picked at mythical pieces of grass supposedly attached to his shirt. 'You know something, Nathan? I've a good mind to make you fall in love with me!' she declared audaciously, and his hand came up and closed around her wrist like a vice.

'I wouldn't attempt it if I were you,' he advised coldly.

Rachel smiled. 'Why not? It could be amusing,' she goaded. It seemed she had hit a nerve! Perhaps he had fallen in love with her already, she mused, then dismissed the idea as preposterous. If there was one man who would never love her, that man was Nathan Wade.

'I will say this only once, sweetheart. Don't try to amuse yourself with me. I make a very bad enemy,' he warned, but she merely smiled at him archly.

'Mmm, a bad enemy but a good lover. What a choice!' Was he protesting a tad too much? No, he was just using his usual tactic of taking a sledge-hammer to crack a nut. 'If you've finished with my hand, I'd like it back,' she added sarcastically.

'We'd better get going,' he said shortly, and made for the pathway. Rachel stared after him ruefully.

He was a man of strong emotions, as she knew to her cost. If he loved as passionately as he hated, the woman he eventually chose would consider herself lucky indeed. It tore her heart in two to know it could never be her. She might be able to incite his passion, but the greater victory of winning his love would always be beyond her reach.

She would have to settle for what she could get, and hope and pray that it wouldn't be the biggest mistake of her life.

CHAPTER EIGHT

DINNER turned out to be a surprisingly formal affair. Luther Ames's guests were expected to dress for the occasion and assemble on the patio for cocktails beforehand. Rachel had chosen to wear one of her new dresses. Floor-length, with a side split that reached above the knee, it's clingy white fabric draped in graceful folds across the bodice, whilst leaving her back bare. She had also put her hair up in a loose knot in the Edwardian style, which allowed fine hairs to escape about her cheeks and neck. At the last minute she had added the diamond necklace to the finished ensemble.

The food had been excellently prepared, and it wasn't hard to imagine that Ames would only accept the best, because it would reflect well on him. Rachel's professional soul drooled at the elaborate concoctions laid before them, and she wondered if she could find a way of having a word with the chef about his truly delicious dessert.

Afterwards they all congregated in the drawing room for coffee and liqueurs, and eventually one of the younger couples switched on the sound system so that they could dance. Rachel had danced with each of the men in turn, and then stood nursing a barely touched margarita, watching Nathan flirt with the buxom brunette who had made such a splash in the pool earlier. The woman was blossoming under his practised charm, and it turned the knife in her heart every time he favoured her with his smile. He looked good enough to eat in his white dinner jacket, and she hated the way the woman kept eyeing him hungrily.

As if he felt her eyes on him, Nathan turned and smiled at her. She smiled back. Of course, she knew what he was doing: proving that she did not have any hold over him. She was sorely tempted to throw her drink in his face, or maybe the brunette's if she continued to hang on his arm like that. Instead she raised her glass to him, then took a much needed sip of its contents.

'Nathan and Anna appear to be enjoying themselves,' Ames observed dryly from behind her, making her jump for she hadn't realised he was there.

Deciding that a jealous response wouldn't go amiss at this point, she scowled. 'Aren't they, though!'

'Do I detect a slight cooling off of the relationship? Have you argued?'

Taking his lead, she turned to him with an aggrieved look. 'Can you believe it? He thinks this dress shows too much of me! We had words on the subject,' she declared huffily, and punctuated the comment with a pointed sniff.

Ames took the opportunity to run his too salacious gaze over her. 'In my humble opinion, you look exquisite,' he returned effusively, and she smiled at him brightly.

'I'll tell you something, Luther, you're a true gentleman. You wouldn't go off and flirt with another woman just because I refused to change, would you?'

'Certainly not. Nathan's a fool. You're worth ten of her,' Ames snorted, at the same time relieving her of her glass and setting it on an end table. 'However, his loss is my gain. Why don't we simply ignore him and get better acquainted?' In a practised move he slipped a proprietorial hand beneath her elbow and led her to the dance floor.

It happened so smoothly Rachel had no time to protest. Before she knew it she was in his arms and being steered across the floor. Ames was a surprisingly good dancer, but she quickly learned he suffered from roving hands. She doubted if there was an inch of her back he hadn't explored, and if she hadn't been doing this in a good cause she would have slapped his face within ten seconds. She put up with it, though his touch made her flesh crawl, and told herself it would be over soon. However, minutes later his hand dropped to her bottom, and she stiffened in outrage. That was going too far. About to remove the offending hand with a pithy command to keep his hands to himself, she was saved by a timely intervention.

'My turn, I think,' Nathan declared suavely, taking her hand from Ames's shoulder and neatly turning her into his own arms. 'You looked as if you needed rescuing,' he remarked when he had steered them out of earshot.

'I did. That man has all the finesse of a ravening octopus!' she said with a shudder.

'Mmm, I thought you were about to hit him, and that wouldn't have helped our cause,' he reminded her coolly, and she narrowed her eyes at him.

'Well, I'm sorry, but I forgot,' she returned snappily. It was all very well for him to remind her of what she was supposed to be doing, but he hadn't had Luther Ames's hands running all over him.

'You forgot? That's a strange thing for you to say,' Nathan charged sardonically, and she stared at him frostily.

'Why? Because you think I'd allow anyone free access to my body? Well, I do have some self-respect, you know. I don't go in for one-night stands, and I don't like men like him mauling me. I detest him touching me. He makes me shudder,' Rachel exclaimed in revulsion, just managing to keep her voice down to an angry hiss.

Nathan looked at her curiously. 'You allow me to touch you,' he said softly, and her eyes locked with his, and her expression softened.

'Yes, well, that's altogether different. You're not a bit like him. I'm not interested in Luther Ames. I never could be,' she declared emphatically, wanting him to know it and believe it.

'But you are interested in me,' he stated thoughtfully.

Rachel smiled into his eyes. 'I thought I'd made that more than obvious this afternoon,' she returned huskily, and the temperature rose significantly in their small corner of the room.

'With what aim in mind?' he asked softly, and she shook her head sadly.

'What a short memory you have. With the aim of getting you into bed, of course,' she reminded him seductively.

'You don't see me as prospective husband material, then?'

That came right out of left field and had her nerves rioting. Of course she saw him as husband material, but it was how *he* saw *her* that counted. Which was why she made her answer light and unconcerned, 'I'm not looking for a husband right now.'

'Just a temporary lover? Someone to tide you over till the next one comes along?' he drawled tauntingly, and though the description stung she shrugged casually.

'You know me. I'm not looking for a soul mate. I certainly wouldn't tie you down.' Not much she wouldn't! Given half a chance she would grab it, but he would never offer her more than a brief affair. He didn't trust her, and he certainly didn't love her. The most they had was a mutual passion. She would make it be enough.

'That's generous of you,' he replied humorously, running a soothing hand down her spine, which caused her to shiver in delight as ripples of pleasure travelled over her from head to toe.

She relaxed immediately, allowing her body to mould itself to his and her head to come to rest on his shoulder. 'You don't know how generous I can be, but you'll find out,' she murmured dreamily, loving the feel of his body moving against hers as they slowly circled the tiny floor.

'I will?' he countered, and she felt the rumble of soft laughter beneath her cheek.

Her free hand stroked the fine cloth of his jacket over his heart. 'Oh, yes. I'm never wrong about these things.'

'You certainly know how to turn a man on,' Nathan returned wryly, and she smiled to herself, for she could feel the response of his body to hers. Combustible, that was what they were. A highly combustible combination.

'Does that mean I'm making progress?' she asked provocatively, moving her hips ever so gently against him, delighting in the tiny growl he couldn't withhold before he eased her away.

'It means we'd better cool it before we cause a minor scandal,' he corrected dryly, and she uttered a husky laugh.

'Mmm, I never was one for spectator sports. Some things are better done in private, where we can let our imaginations run riot,' she flirted, wondering at her own daring, yet knowing she wouldn't stop now for anything on earth.

Nathan's blue eyes scorched her from a distance. 'I imagine you have one hell of an imagination!'

Reaching out, she brushed one fingertip softly over his bottom lip. 'Just say the word and you'll find out.'

'No charge?'

Her eyes held his solemnly. 'Never for you,' she said gruffly, unable to joke about that. What she had to give would be given freely. With love.

A tiny frown creased his brow at her seriousness.

'Sometimes there's something about you that doesn't quite fit. I can't work out what it is,' he said slowly, and she couldn't resist smoothing out that frown with her thumb.

'Don't worry about it. I'm sure if it's important it will come to you. If not…well, what difference will it make?' she declared philosophically.

'None, I guess,' he returned, though he didn't sound too convinced.

The music ended and she moved away from him reluctantly. 'Take my word for it. You were right when you said we are what we are. I am what you see.'

He shook his head in a vague gesture of dissatisfaction. 'Exactly. You are what I see, but what *do* I see?'

His strange mood disquieted her, and she forced a tinkling laugh from a suddenly tight throat. 'There's no mystery about that. You see a woman you want. She isn't perfect, but she never pretended to be.'

'No, you're not perfect. In fact, now I come to think of it, you've never made any attempt to hide how imperfect you are since I told you about Antibes,' he enlarged thoughtfully.

Rachel could feel her pulse beating more quickly in her throat. Did this mean she had got through to him by the lake, after all? 'Maybe that's because you've been so determined to think the worst of me.'

Nathan paused for a split second, but then shook his head. 'For a moment you almost convinced me

I've been imagining things…but I can't doubt the evidence of my own eyes, now, can I?'

His utter implacability made her shiver, and for once she was glad to see Luther Ames bearing down on them. It brought to an end a conversation which had been heading in unexpected and hopeful directions, but which had then been brought back on track with a vengeance.

'I'm glad to see you two have made it up,' Ames declared with heavy-handed bonhomie. 'But I'm going to have to steal Nathan away from you, my dear Rachel. It's time we got down to the serious business of the day. If you're ready, Nathan?'

Nathan nodded. 'I'm always ready for a good game of poker.'

'Then we will be sure to oblige you,' Ames replied smoothly.

Rachel quickly slipped her arm through Nathan's. 'Let's hope I can bring you luck again, darling.'

'I'm afraid that will be impossible. We take the game very seriously here, and non-players are not allowed in the room,' Ames refused politely.

She favoured him with a cajoling smile. 'Oh, but I only want to watch. I won't be any trouble.'

'I'm sure you won't, angel, nevertheless you will have to remain here with the other ladies. I'm sure you can find something to talk about to pass the time,' he said firmly.

With something approaching a flounce she released Nathan's arm.

'Looks like you're on your own this time, darling.' She pouted, then placed her hands on his shoulders and raised herself on tiptoe. 'But here's something for luck,' she added, taking his lips in a sizzling kiss that raised her own temperature and brought a flash of fire to Nathan's eyes.

'Something tells me I can't lose,' he declared a trifle thickly. 'Keep it hot for me, darling, and we'll carry on from where we left off later,' he commanded, before turning and walking away with Ames.

As soon as the men left the party, the fizz went out of the evening. The other women were clearly used to being abandoned to their own devices, and quickly found various ways of amusing themselves. None were inclined to engage Rachel in conversation, and she wasn't altogether sorry. She had nothing in common with them, and besides, she had more important things to do. This was the perfect opportunity to search Ames's rooms.

She didn't leave immediately, though. She spent half an hour glancing through a fashion magazine, then tossed it aside with a sigh of impatience. 'This is boring,' she declared to the room at large. 'How long are they going to be?'

The brunette glanced up from filing her nails. 'Hours.'

'It could go on to sun-up,' a young blonde added long-sufferingly.

'That's nothing,' one of the others put in. 'I've known a poker game to last three or four days.'

Rachel glanced from one to the other in curiosity, for none of them sounded unduly put out. 'Don't you get fed up waiting?' she asked, knowing that she would never stand for it.

The brunette waggled a hand dripping with diamonds. 'It has its compensations,' she declared dryly, and the others laughed with her. 'You'll get used to it. You have to if you don't want to kill the goose that lays the golden eggs.'

Rachel grinned, though the avariciousness of the woman horrified her. 'I see what you mean. Oh, well, in that case I think I'll go and have a long soak in the tub,' she announced, climbing to her feet. By the time she reached the door they were all back in their own tiny worlds again.

Raising her eyebrows in amazement, Rachel left them to it. Outside, she paused to listen, but the house was silent. Climbing the stairs, she ignored the hallway on the right, which led to their room, and headed left. If anyone found her where she wasn't supposed to be she could always claim to have got lost.

Retracing the route they had taken earlier in the day, she mounted the tower stairs until she came to the door to Ames's study. With her hand on the doorknob, she took a deep breath, then turned it. To her relief the door opened soundlessly and she slipped inside, closing it quickly behind her. She took a second to adjust her eyes to the gloom, then made her way to the desk. Moonlight streamed through the windows, giving her more than enough light to see by.

The desk drawers were unlocked, and it was the work of a moment to shuffle through the contents.

The letters weren't there. Cursing silently, she straightened up and glanced round the room. There were several pictures on the walls and she went to them all in turn, checking for a wall safe. She found it behind the second to last one and stared at it helplessly. Great. She had found the safe, but there was no way of opening it. If the letters were inside, they were stymied.

Still, whilst she was there she might as well check out Ames's bedroom. It was on the next floor and she entered it uneasily. Just being there made her feel creepy. There was no light in this room, and she realised heavy drapes had been pulled over the window, which meant she could safely turn on the light. Telling herself not to be so sensitive, she set about systematically searching the room. The man possessed an amazing number of suits, and she felt bound to go through all the pockets. Fruitlessly, as it turned out. The dresser proved negative too, as did the highboy. It was almost as an afterthought that she checked the bedside table, and it was there that she found what she sought when she opened the top drawer. Two small piles of envelopes, with addresses penned in the same forceful hand.

Rachel could scarcely believe her luck, but there they were. Delighted to have had success so quickly, she picked up one pile, then hesitated with her hand hovering over the other. The only reason they could be in Ames's drawer was because he was using the letters as bedtime reading. If she took them now, he was sure to miss them. The sensible thing to do would be to leave the letters where they were and retrieve them in the morning before they left. That way they would have at least a day before Ames discovered they were gone.

Reluctantly she put the letters back again, and closed the drawer. She hated to leave them but there was no other way. Taking a swift glance round to make sure that nothing was out of place, she turned out the light and made her way back downstairs. This time she took the hallway to her room, and only breathed easily again when she was inside it with the door closed.

All she had to do now was wait for Nathan to return, which apparently could be anything between an hour and four days! The prospect did not delight her, for she hated waiting at the best of times. Now, with success within their grasp, it was even more irritating.

Declaring her intention of having a long soak in the tub had been a ruse for leaving the group, but as time passed she decided she might as well do it anyway. It didn't look as if Nathan was going to come to bed any time soon. So she took a long, relaxing bath and washed her hair, slipped on her nightdress, then curled up on top of the bed to wait.

At first the imminence of Nathan's return and their having to share the bed, had her nerves dancing in anticipation. She thought up various ways of getting him to drop his guard and make love to her, but as the hours passed the likelihood of it ever happening grew more remote, and eventually the glow of expectancy vanished altogether. Disappointed, she pulled a pillow free and cuddled up to it. The silence deepened and her eyelids dropped. She recalled hearing a clock somewhere in the house striking two a.m., and was unable to keep sleep at bay any longer.

Nathan found her curled up amongst the pillows when he entered the room somewhere around dawn. Tossing his jacket on a chair, he kicked off his shoes and tugged his tie free, sending it to join his jacket. Crossing the room, for a moment he stood at the side of the bed looking down at her in the soft glow of the bedside lamp, a strange, brooding expression in his eyes.

'Oh, hell,' he swore, and with a resigned sigh sat on the edge of the bed and reached across to run a finger along the fragile curve of her cheek.

Rachel sighed and came awake, blinking sleepily up at him. Realising who it was, and with her defences down, her lips curved into a welcoming smile. 'Hi,' she greeted in a sleepy voice, pushing her tumbled hair out of her eyes. 'What time is it?'

Nathan didn't bother looking at his watch. 'The sun's coming up,' he supplied softly, brushing a lock of hair away from her chin and watching it settle like a golden halo on the pillow.

Still more than half asleep, Rachel frowned. 'Have you been playing all this time?' she asked in disapproval, and Nathan smiled.

'You sound like my mother. You don't look like her, though,' he added whimsically, allowing his eyes to rove over her relaxed body, not missing the expanse of thigh where her nightie had worked up as she slept.

Of course at that Rachel's body lurched back into tingling life, and the dregs of sleep vanished rapidly.

'How *do* I look?' she asked, more than a little breathlessly, feeling her blood starting to course thickly through her body.

'Soft, warm and sexy,' he responded hotly, sending her heart leaping into her throat. The heat in his gaze started a throbbing way down deep inside her.

'You must be tired!' she exclaimed in amusement.

'Not that tired,' he countered, and she wondered if he really knew what message he was sending out. He sounded like a man intent on making love, which was a complete about-face.

She pointed a finger at him. 'Nathan Wade, this is not like you. If I didn't know better, I'd say you were trying to seduce me,' she reproved mockingly, whilst holding her breath lest he change his mind yet again.

Reaching out, he took her hand, expression wry. 'Don't you want to be seduced?' he asked, playing with her fingers.

'Has something hit you on the head?' she countered.

To her surprise he pulled a face. 'You could say that. It struck me when I looked at you just now. I wondered what the hell I was fighting this attraction for. I want you; you want me. You were right. We're not talking about love here. This is sex, pure and simple. The surest way to get you out of my system is to let it run its course.'

Rachel took a steadying breath and kept her eyes on their joined hands. He made it sound so cold, so clinical, and her heart tightened painfully. Yet this was what she wanted, because it was all there could be.

'How long do you think it will take?' she asked through a painfully tight throat, and he shrugged.

'To have enough of each other? A week. A month. I'm sure you'll tell me when you've found somebody else,' he declared with heavy irony, and her eyes lifted to his face.

'What about you? You must tell me when the next woman catches your eye. I wouldn't want to outstay my welcome,' she said easily, though the words were like bitter gall on her tongue. She hated the thought of her successor already, and their affair hadn't even started.

Blue eyes met green, and was it her imagination or did she see resignation there in the instant before he smiled? 'You can count on it,' he declared lazily, bending his head and placing a trail of kisses along her arm. She caught her breath as he found the tender inner skin of her elbow, stroking it with the very tip of his tongue, and all sensible thought left her. There was only Nathan, and the knowledge that, for now, he was hers.

Her free hand combed its way into his hair, loving the silky thickness of it and the way it clung to her fingers. In one smooth movement he stretched himself out on the bed beside her and took her in his arms. As she curled her own around his neck she promised herself that no matter what happened after tonight she would have no regrets.

That first time there was no room for finesse. The

need they shared, having been contained so long, was too strong for moderation, and from their first kiss passion flared out of control. It was as if a dam had broken, and the floodwaters of desire swept them away. Each kiss was hotter than the last, each caress drew sighs and moans of intense pleasure. Clothes were ripped away by impatient fingers, and when flesh touched flesh it was almost more than they could stand. Free from that final restriction, caressing hands explored silken skin, and lips followed. It was heady and arousing, and Rachel could feel her limbs turning molten, her breasts swelling into aching globes that welcomed the attention of burning male lips. His tongue caressed her relentlessly, until her body arched against his in silent supplication. She could feel his arousal and wanted to have the strength of him inside her. Only that would make her feel complete.

Her hands moved restlessly over the satin smoothness of his back, finding his flanks and holding him to her as she writhed beneath him. When he parted her legs and slipped between them she groaned, and when he lifted her and thrust into her Nathan's groan echoed hers. He went still, trying to prolong the moment, but the need was too great and control was a thing of the past. Rachel held on tight as they moved together, welcoming each deepening thrust that raised them to unscaled heights of pleasure. It couldn't last, and with a cry her head went back and she plunged over the edge, taking Nathan with her mere seconds later.

Aeons later the world re-imposed itself on their

shattered bodies. Pulse rates settled back into a normal rhythm. But for Rachel everything had changed. Nothing could have prepared her for what they had just shared, and she knew that nothing could ever replace it. Nathan was heavy on top of her, but she didn't mind. She welcomed his weight, for she wanted to remember everything about tonight. Every touch, every sigh.

Eventually, though, Nathan roused, moving off her. For a split second she felt bereft, then his arms reached out for her, drawing her into his side. Her heart swelled and ached as she wished he could love her but accepted that he wouldn't. Swallowing a huge ball of emotion, she rested her head over his heart and allowed sleep to take her.

CHAPTER NINE

WHEN Rachel awoke the second time she was alone in the bed and sunlight streamed through the window. For one instant she imagined she had dreamt the events of the night, but the protestation of her muscles as she sat up told her it had all been real. Nathan's clothes were gone, but her nightie was draped across the foot of the bed and she reached for it, slipping it on just as the bathroom door opened and Nathan walked in clad only in a pair of shorts.

Fresh from the shower, he looked healthy and vibrant, and instantly her mouth went dry. He halted when he saw that she was awake, his eyes running lazily over her love-bruised lips, the only visible sign of their shared passion.

'Good morning,' he greeted her easily, and she shivered faintly at his lack of emotion. She wasn't sure what she had expected, but his matter-of-factness wasn't it. How could he be so cool after what they had shared? she wondered. The obvious answer hurt. He could be cool because last night had been nothing special for him.

She realised then that she had been harbouring the secret hope that, having made love to her, he would suddenly and miraculously love her. As far as Nathan was concerned, though, nothing had

changed, and it would be in her own best interests
to act as if it was the same for her.

'Good morning. I hope you haven't used up all
the hot water,' she remarked lightly as she scram-
bled off the bed.

That nerve ticked in Nathan's jaw as he turned to
the closet and selected a pair of trousers and a shirt
which he proceeded to put on. 'There's plenty. Help
yourself.'

Rachel stared at his back, feeling the urge to say
something, yet unable to produce a word. If he'd
just taken her in his arms for a second she wouldn't
have felt nearly so chilled. But she could hardly expect it, for he had told her himself theirs wasn't a
love affair.

'Is something wrong?' Nathan asked when he
turned and discovered her still standing there.

She jumped nervily and hurried to her own closet,
taking clothes at random. 'Nothing's wrong,' she
lied, when in actuality everything was. She supposed
she would get used to it—in about ten or twenty
years. Scuttling like a turtle, she vanished into the
sanctuary of the bathroom.

The stinging shower revived her, returning some
sense of calm. She had known how it was going to
be, she told herself, so there was no point in getting
upset. Turning off the water, she stepped out of the
cubicle and reached for a towel. At all costs she
must never reveal that he meant any more to her
than she obviously did to him. She must be the epit-
ome of cool. Drying herself briskly, she dressed in
the purely lucky selection of cotton trousers and a

vest-style tee-shirt. Taking several deep breaths, she felt more prepared to face him.

Nathan was standing by the window when she re-entered the room, and he turned to her immediately. 'How are you feeling?' he surprised her by asking, and she frowned.

'Fine. I feel fine. Why shouldn't I be?' she returned with a slightly stilted laugh.

'I don't know,' he countered. 'You just appear to be acting a little oddly.'

Her nerves jumped, and she told herself she would have to be more careful in future. 'You're imagining things. Put it down to hunger, if you must. I'm ravenous. I feel as if I could eat a horse!' she exclaimed, only belatedly realising the implications of what she had said. Her eyes shot to his and met a look of amusement.

'I'm not surprised. You don't hold back, do you?'

Colour made up of part embarrassment, part-annoyance stained her cheeks. 'Would you rather that I had?'

'Not at all,' he denied with a shake of the head.

'Good. Because I don't recall you holding back, either.'

His lips twitched. 'In which case we'll need two horses for breakfast,' he teased. 'One for you and one for me.'

She raised an eyebrow at that. 'You didn't give that impression just now,' she pointed out, recalling how chilled he had made her feel.

'Didn't I?' he returned sardonically. 'Perhaps that was because I was fighting the urge to climb right back into bed with you,' he added, stealing her breath away with the heat that now positively blazed from his eyes.

She licked her lips, and at once his eyes dropped to her mouth. 'Why didn't you?' she challenged, sounding huskily seductive to her own ears.

Nathan dragged a hand through his still damp hair, leaving it rakishly tousled. 'God, you are pure temptation!' he exclaimed, sounding not in the least disappointed to know it. 'Behave yourself, Rachel. We still have the letters to find, remember?'

She hadn't been deliberately provocative, but it delighted her to know that he thought she had been. Now that she looked more closely, she realised that under the surface he wasn't nearly as cool as he looked. She hugged the knowledge to her and rather belatedly recalled what she had intended telling him last night, before they'd got distracted.

'There's no need. I've found them,' she told him triumphantly. 'Whilst you were playing cards I searched Luther's study. I didn't find them there, but I did find them in the drawer of his bedside table. I think he reads them every night before he goes to sleep!'

'It sounds like the sort of thing he would do!' Nathan remarked scornfully. 'Where are the letters now? Did you put them somewhere safe?'

'I left them where they were,' she said, and hastened to explain when he frowned. 'I didn't want him to find them missing last night. I thought we could get them this morning, then, if we left, he wouldn't discover they were gone until tonight.'

Nathan grinned at her. 'You'd make a good spy,' he observed approvingly, but Rachel shuddered.

'My nerves couldn't stand it. This is the closest I ever want to come to anything underhand.'

'Fortunately it will all be over soon. It's just as well I lost last night. Ames won't be surprised by our sudden decision to leave,' Nathan mused thoughtfully, whilst Rachel latched onto the one salient point.

'You *lost*?' she charged in disbelief.

A muscle tightened in his jaw. 'Don't sound so surprised. People do lose, you know.'

'Yes,' she agreed, 'but you told me you never lose.'

'Apparently I was wrong,' he retorted tetchily. 'Let's not make an issue of it. The thing is, we can use it to our advantage. It gives us a valid reason for leaving. After breakfast you'll have to keep Ames busy whilst I go and retrieve the letters. We'll leave as soon as I get back. Think you can manage that?'

'Of course.' Rachel nodded, mightily relieved that they would be leaving soon.

Nathan smiled at her approvingly. 'Good. We'd better pack now so we won't have to delay our departure later. Just for the record, I wouldn't have wanted anyone else helping me on this job,' he told her seriously, and she smiled back at him a trifle diffidently. It wouldn't keep her warm at night, but all the same it was nice to know.

'I'm glad I came, too. But I won't be sorry to leave, either. If I never see Luther Ames again after

today it will be too soon,' she pronounced and, as
Nathan had intended, quite forgot about the amazing
fact that he had lost at cards.

As Nathan had suggested, Ames wasn't at all surprised when they told him they were going to leave
after breakfast. He had the smugly self-satisfied look
of a man who had bested his rival—in cards, at least.

'I'll need to use your telephone to book our flights
back home.' Nathan expanded their tale, and Rachel
saw an opening and took it.

'Home? But you promised me we'd go shopping!'
she protested loudly.

'Sorry, sweetheart, but shopping is out. You can
blame Luther here for taking me to the cleaners,'
Nathan returned wryly, playing along.

She turned a cold shoulder on him and folded her
arms huffily. 'I don't see why I have to suffer just
because you lost at a silly game of cards.'

'Next time, darling,' Nathan promised as he rose
from the table. He bent down to kiss her cheek, but
she jerked away from him.

'I'm not so sure there will be a next time,' she
pouted, whereupon Nathan shrugged.

'Please yourself. I'm going inside to book our
flights and pack. We should be ready to leave in
half an hour.'

Rachel sniffed. 'Don't rush on my account!' she
retorted coldly, and Ames dropped a soothing hand
on her shoulder.

'Don't worry, Nathan. I'll look after her for you,'
he declared smoothly, and after exchanging a brief

but significant look with Rachel, Nathan walked away.

As soon as he'd disappeared Ames stood and slipped a hand through Rachel's arm, urging her to her feet. 'Come along, angel, let's you and I go for a walk. Perhaps I can think of a way to cheer you up.'

She pretended to perk up, shooting him a provocative smile. 'I'm open to any reasonable offer.' Lord, she hoped Nathan wouldn't be long. She wasn't sure how long she could keep this up.

Ames smiled, his eyes roving over her hungrily. 'I thought you might be. You know, you don't have to leave with Nathan. I can give you anything your heart desires.'

Rachel feigned enthusiasm, whilst she had an uneasy feeling about the turn the conversation was taking. 'Do you mean it? You'll take me shopping?'

He laughed, a rather unpleasant sound as far as Rachel was concerned. 'You can shop till you drop.'

Feeling nauseous, she glanced at him from beneath her lashes. 'You make it hard for a girl to say no,' she giggled. Where are you, Nathan? she called out silently.

Their stroll had brought them to a small arbour set beside the path, and it was here that Ames stopped and turned her to face him. 'Then say yes,' he urged, running his hands up and down her arms.

Rachel just caught back a telling shudder in time. 'Maybe I will. I'll have to think about it,' she prevaricated, and his eyes narrowed in quick annoyance.

'What's to think about? Nathan's a loser and you know it. Why else would you have been coming on to me ever since we met?'

'I have not!' she gasped, pretending to be affronted. Now would be a good time for you to turn up, Nathan, she told his absent figure telepathically.

Ames's smile was dripping with confidence. 'Of course you have, angel. Stop giving me the runaround. We both know you're going to stay, so how about giving me a little something in advance, hmm?'

Before she could protest, Rachel found herself clasped in a pair of surprisingly strong arms. Then his mouth came down on hers so hard his teeth cut her lip, and she tasted blood. She tried to break free, but Ames was much stronger than she would have imagined. Feeling him trying to insinuate his tongue into her mouth, she began to struggle in earnest. Her efforts only made him laugh, and she panicked a little then. She didn't want him to kiss her or touch her or do any of the things he was doing, but with her arms pinioned by his there was little she could do until he stopped for breath, and then she quickly bit down on his lip as hard as she could.

With a howl of pain Ames thrust her away from him with such force she stumbled and fell, hitting her cheek on the arbour seat. Slightly stunned, she couldn't take advantage of her freedom and escape.

Ames's fingers probed his mouth and the stared at he blood on his hand. The expression in his eyes turned nasty and he took an angry step towards her.

'Why, you damned little tease!' he growled threateningly, but got no further.

'What the hell is going on here?' Nathan's frosty question had never been more welcome—at least to Rachel. 'Are you OK, sweetheart?' he asked her, helping her to her feet, his expression clouding when he saw the cut on her lip and the graze on her cheek.

Pure relief brought real tears to her eyes, and she flung her arms around his neck. 'Oh, Nathan, I want to go home!' she cried, and meant it.

Nathan's arms automatically tightened protectively around her, and the look he sent Ames was glacial. 'We are going home, darling, that's why I came to get you. But first you have to tell me if he hurt you.'

The uncompromising tone of his voice had her blinking at him mistily. There wasn't a doubt in her mind that if she said yes he would gather great satisfaction from punching Ames's lights out. But however much she might want to see the man laid out cold, she had to be honest.

'He didn't really hurt me. I fell and hit the seat.'

Nathan searched her eyes then nodded, satisfied she had told the truth. 'You're lucky, Ames,' he declared with quiet menace. 'Very lucky. Nobody manhandles my woman.'

The other man gathered his composure with a visible effort. 'Apparently not, though she gave me every impression that she would welcome my attention. The woman's a tease.' he accused, and Nathan smiled.

'I know. That's part of her charm. Come along, Rachel, I think it's about time we left.'

They retraced their steps along the path, leaving Ames staring wrathfully after them. He made no attempt to follow them, though Rachel felt his daggers in her back all the way until they rounded a bend and vanished from his sight. Only then did she breathe a little easier.

'Did you get them?' she asked as they approached the house and skirted round it. 'Were they all there?'

'I hope so. They're safely locked in my suitcase, at all events.' They reached the car and Nathan held the passenger door open for her to climb in. Then he took his own seat, and within minutes they were driving away.

Halfway to the town of Crystal Bay, Nathan pulled the car to the side of the road and shut off the engine. Rachel glanced over at him in surprise.

'What's wrong?' Had they forgotten something? The last thing she wanted to do was return to Ames's house.

Nathan said nothing, but, reaching out a hand, tipped her head so that he could see the graze on her cheek. A bruise was already starting to form, but he touched her so gently she scarcely felt it. 'The skin's not broken, but we'll clean it up when we get to the airport. I hate to have to say it, but you're probably going to have a black eye.'

'Oh, no!' she exclaimed in dismay, and his smile was wry.

''Fraid so. Look at it this way: it will be an interesting conversation piece,' he teased, then his eye rediscovered the cut on her lip and the smile vanished. 'Now *that* wasn't made by a fall.'

'No,' she admitted, her tongue probing the sore spot.

His thumb brushed the small wound. 'Care to tell me what happened?' It wasn't so much a question as a command, and Rachel recognised that even as she silently marvelled at the unexpected protective note in his voice. It made her feel strangely bubbly and warm inside.

'It really wasn't anything very much. Ames tried to win me away from you, and thought a kiss would help. I disagreed. The cut on *his* lip is much worse than this,' she added with a reminiscent smile.

Surprise and amusement chased across his face. 'You bit him?'

'I have very sharp teeth.'

Nathan laughed softly. 'I'll have to remember that.'

'Oh, I wouldn't bite you,' Rachel was quick to point out. 'I just happen to be choosy about who kisses me.'

Blue eyes dropped to her lips. 'So, if I were to kiss you now, you wouldn't complain?'

Her pulse kick-started into life and raced into another gear. 'I'd more likely complain if you didn't,' she said with soft expectancy.

Nathan dipped his head and took her lips in a kiss so gentle it could have been the brush of a butterfly's wing. 'Better?' he asked, sitting back, and she had to swallow a large lump of emotion in order to form an answer.

'Much better.'

'I should never have left you alone with him,' he said next, in self-condemnation, but Rachel quickly shook her head and smiled.

'It wasn't your fault, and besides, it was worth it to get the letters. To think of him reading them— and making millions using them to blackmail his own aunt—makes me want to shudder. What I want to do now is get them back to Grandfather as quickly as possible, so that he can hand them back to his friend.'

'I'm with you on that. We'll put in a call to him from the airport, telling him they're on their way,' Nathan proposed as he restarted the car and set it in motion. 'With luck and a following wind, she should have the letters back some time tomorrow morning.'

It was in the early hours of the following morning, London time, by the time they landed, and Rachel was exhausted. She had wanted to be there when Nathan handed the letters over to her grandfather, but when he suggested that the taxi drop her off at her flat first she put up very little argument. Instructing the taxi driver to wait, Nathan helped her stack her luggage in the lift.

'Do you want me to come up with you?' he asked, and though she would have loved to have said yes she was awake enough to know that Emma would be home. Her cousin often stayed up into the small hours, and she couldn't take the chance on them meeting before she had had time to explain the truth to Nathan. She had abandoned the idea of throwing that truth in his face now that they were lovers, but that didn't mean the truth wouldn't have a cataclys-mic effect.

'No, I can manage from here,' she refused reluc-tantly. 'You take the letters to Grandfather. Despite the time, he'll be waiting up for you. Tell him I'll see him tomorrow.'

'I will,' he promised, then hesitated for a long moment when she thought—hoped—he would kiss her. Instead, with a brush of his knuckles along her jaw, he turned towards the door and the waiting taxi.

Rachel watched him go in disappointment. The least he could have done was kiss her, she thought wistfully. Then, even as she watched, he halted in the doorway and cast a look at her over his shoulder. That nerve ticked in his jaw as he abruptly turned and strode back to her, his hand snaking out to cap-ture the back of her neck and draw her face to his.

'I don't know who needs this more,' he growled passionately, and took her lips in a searing kiss that left her aching for more the instant his lips left hers again. 'Sweet dreams, Rachel,' he wished her gruffly, and this time he walked away and didn't turn back.

With a sigh she pressed the button for her floor, knowing at least that Nathan hadn't wanted to walk away any more than she had wanted him to. It gave her a warm glow inside as she ferried her cases to the door of her flat, then let herself in.

As expected, Emma was still stretched out on the couch watching TV, and glanced up in surprise when the door opened. 'Rachel? I didn't expect you back so soon!' she exclaimed, coming to help Rachel with her cases. 'You look bushed,' she observed, once she had had a closer look at her cousin.

Rachel smiled weakly, glad to sink down on her own comfortable couch. 'It was a hectic couple of days, but we got the letters back. Nathan's taking them to Grandfather now.'

'So you didn't end up throttling each other, I take it?' Emma teased, and her eyebrows rose when she saw the betraying colour enter Rachel's averted cheeks. 'Oh, no! Tell me you didn't!' she exclaimed in dismay, and Rachel avoided her eyes.

'I don't know what you're talking about,' she lied, knowing very well, and hating her inability to hide anything from her cousin.

'Oh, yes, you do!' Emma countered. 'You went to bed with him, didn't you?' she charged bluntly, deepening the betraying colour tellingly.

'There was only one bed,' Rachel pointed out faintly, but that only drew a snort of derision.

'You can't distract me that way, Rachel. How could you do it, when you promised me faithfully you would come back unscathed?'

Rachel folded her arms defensively. 'I am unscathed,' she insisted, but Emma sent her a sceptical look.

'Are you telling me Nathan Wade suddenly discovered he was madly in love with you?' she charged with cutting directness, and Rachel's throat closed over.

'No. He doesn't love me,' she admitted gruffly.

'He wants me, although he doesn't really want to do that either,' she added with brutal honesty.

'So he still doesn't know the truth about Antibes?'

Rachel shook her head tiredly. 'I did try, but there wasn't time to convince him properly. Everything happened so fast. But don't worry. I am going to tell him.'

'When?' Emma wanted to know, and Rachel winced.

'As soon as I think the moment is right.'

Emma didn't look happy, but she knew when to let the matter drop. 'Just don't leave it too long. The longer you leave it, the more of a fool he's going to feel.'

'Yes, Mama!'

Emma held up her hands. 'OK, I won't say another word. I just hope you know what you're doing,' she added disapprovingly. 'Do you want me to run a bath for you, or do you want to eat first?'

As if that was a cue, Rachel yawned widely and stretched tired limbs. 'We ate on the plane, and it was surprisingly good. All I want now is a bath and my bed. I feel as if I could sleep for a week!'

'Come on, then,' Emma urged. 'You get out of those clothes whilst I run the bath.'

Rachel enjoyed a deliciously relaxing bath, then fell into bed and was asleep in minutes. When she did finally stir, the morning was well advanced. She had intended visiting her grandfather much earlier, but knew he wouldn't mind if she was late. The doorbell rang whilst she was still in bed, and she heard Emma answer it. Not long afterwards the door closed again, and she guessed it was one of their neighbours come to borrow something.

Her stomach growled loudly, reminding her it was ages since she had eaten, so she climbed out of bed, slipping on the silk robe her grandmother had brought back with her from a trip to Hong Kong many years ago now. Still tying the belt, with fingers that felt like thumbs, she padded out of the bedroom in search of food.

'Who was that at the door, Emma?' she asked as she walked into the living room. The strained silence struck her at once, and she glanced up in swift alarm.

'The last person you were expecting,' Nathan replied softly, and after a stunned moment of intense surprise Rachel closed her eyes, knowing that the sky had just fallen in.

CHAPTER TEN

'N-NATHAN! Wh-what a surprise!' she stammered
stupidly, her heart sinking when she looked at him
again and saw the forbidding expression on his face.
'He—er—came to take you to your grandfather,'
Emma explained tonelessly, looking from one to the
other.

'Linus wanted to thank you himself,' Nathan
added shortly. 'I promised I would pick you up as
early as possible.'

Rachel's fingers tied themselves into a nervous
knot. 'I see,' she responded lamely, unable to think
of a sensible thing to say with Nathan's contained
anger turning the air in the room electric. The reason
for it was simple. As she had feared, one glance at
Emma and he had recognised her.

Nathan's jaw clenched, and his next words
backed up her guess. 'Imagine my surprise when
this young woman opened the door. She was the
very last person I expected to see. Correct me if I'm
wrong, but she looks a hell of a lot like the woman
in Antibes,' he ground out with restrained anger.
'The one you played merry hell with!'

'You're not wrong, Mr Wade. I was in Antibes
that summer,' Emma answered him smoothly, and
he shot her a narrow look.

'And now you turn up here! What a small world!
I think it's about time one of you started to do some

explaining!' he ordered scathingly, looking directly at Rachel.

Before she could answer, however, Emma spoke up again. 'Its really very simple, Mr Wade. Rachel went to Antibes to save me from a fortune-hunter. We're a very close family, and she knows I would do the same for her. The methods she used were extreme, but they worked where all else had failed.'

It was clear to the cousins that Nathan battled with seething emotions. He sought confirmation. 'So you're telling me that what I saw was nothing more than an act?'

Emma nodded. 'Staged to trap a trickster, nobody else.'

He turned and took a couple of steps away. Hands on hips, head bowed, he digested what he had been told. Eventually he took a deep breath and faced them again, his expression composed, but Rachel didn't believe for a moment that he had stopped being angry—at least, not with her.

'So, who exactly are you?'

Finding her voice at last, Rachel made the introduction. 'She's my cousin, Emma. You've heard me talk about her. We run the catering business together,' she explained, and watched uneasily as Nathan coolly shook Emma's hand. He was too calm. Far too calm.

'I'm pleased to meet you at last, Emma, though the circumstances are not quite what I expected.' Nathan greeted her with a friendly smile, but Rachel was quick to note that his eyes were distinctly unfriendly when they glanced her way.

'I'm sorry it happened this way, too,' Emma responded calmly. 'It isn't how I would have wanted it. But, having said that, you must accept some of the blame.'

Nathan looked a trifle taken aback at that. 'Is that so?'

'Oh, yes. To continue to think the way you do about my cousin once you got to know her is something I will always find hard to forgive,' Emma reproved him.

Comprehending from her remarks that Emma was fully aware of his assumptions regarding Rachel, Nathan set his hands on his hips and smiled tigerishly. 'Perpetuating the lie isn't something I find easy to forgive either,' he growled, rounding on Rachel. 'Now I understand why you were so anxious I didn't come here. You didn't want me to see Emma and discover the number you were doing on me. You've been playing me for a fool all along, haven't you, Rachel? Were you ever going to tell me, I wonder?' he demanded, looking her squarely in the eye, chilling her blood with the iciness of his gaze.

Emma held up a hand hastily at this point. 'Ah, this is where I leave. It sounds to me like its going to be the death of a thousand cuts, and if you don't mind I'd rather not witness the blood being spilled.' Giving her cousin a mixed apologetic and reassuring look, she disappeared into her own bedroom.

Left alone with Nathan, Rachel folded her arms protectively about her waist and braced herself for the storm she knew was about to hit her. 'Of course I was going to tell you. If you remember, I did try,' she explained staunchly, and winced inwardly when she saw his eyes narrow dangerously.

'Try?' he scoffed scornfully. 'Don't give me that, Rachel. You could have said something more to me when I *first* told you what I believed about you!' he added hotly, and that struck home, because she had known at the time she was making an error. She just hadn't known how big a one.

Knowing she was at fault was one thing, but he wasn't faultless either, and that brought her chin up defiantly, 'No, I couldn't. You'd made me too damned angry. My God, how do you think I felt, knowing precisely what you had thought of me all that time?' she exclaimed in a choked voice. 'I knew you despised me, but I never knew why until then. Damn it, Nathan, how could you think I was like that?' she accused painfully.

His jaw tensed so hard she expected it to break. 'Very easily, after what I saw.'

Hurt brought angry moisture to her eyes and she blinked it away hastily. 'But you only ever saw me act that way *once*! Didn't I deserve the benefit of the doubt when we met and you saw me as a totally different person?'

His expression set mutinously. 'How was I to know you weren't playing more tricks? The truth would have helped, of course. Maybe I was hasty. Maybe I should have questioned more. But it doesn't alter the fact you should have told me the truth at the outset,' he pointed out coldly, and the injustice of it made her mad.

'You wouldn't have believed me! Don't you dare try to deny it, Nathan, because you know you wouldn't. You had this fixed idea about me and you refused to let it go no matter what I said. No matter how many times I tried to tell you that there was an innocent explanation and that you didn't know me, you insisted that you did,' Rachel countered angrily.

His nostrils flared as he drew in an angry breath. 'So you decided to make a fool of me instead?' Nathan accused, and she swallowed hard, her throat painfully tight with the emotions ripping through her.

'Yes, at first. I wanted to pay you back for all the things you had said. I was going to throw the truth in your face when we had got the letters back,' she confessed hardily, and saw that nerve begin to tick away in his jaw.

'So why didn't you? You had ample opportunity after we left Ames's house,' he demanded, and, caught out by the direction this was going, she hastily dropped her gaze to the floor.

'I changed my mind,' she said gruffly, protecting herself with half of the truth, and he uttered a harsh bark of laughter.

'Sure you did! You thought it would be more fun to let me find out this way!'

Looking up swiftly, Rachel shook her head in vehement denial. 'No! I didn't plan this. I changed my mind because...' She hesitated, knowing she was skating on dangerous ground. 'Because I didn't want to damage our relationship,' she admitted huskily, her eyes searching his, hoping to see some softening there. In vain.

'Relationship?' Nathan exclaimed scornfully, unwittingly tearing at her fragile heart. 'We don't have a relationship, sweetheart. We spent one night together, that was all.'

That he could reduce the passion between them to those terms didn't bode well, but still she tried to salvage something from the mess. 'It wasn't just one night. It was a beginning. What we feel when we're together isn't over.' It was there now, hidden behind the anger.

'Maybe not,' he agreed tautly. 'But if you think I want any more to do with you after this, you're sadly mistaken!'

Rachel had always known that he would not take the truth well; that was why she had wanted their affair to have lasted longer than one day. For then it would have had some hopes of riding the storm. It had been a faint hope at best, but it was all she had had. She had wanted more time. Had wanted memories to see her through the dark times. But there were to be none, and it hurt so much she could only respond with anger and scorn for what he was throwing away in his hypocrisy.

'So that's it? Is all over because your *pride* is hurt that I didn't tell you about Emma. Well, what about *my* pride? You jumped to conclusions about me and hung onto them like grim death! Do you have any idea how much that hurt me?' she charged him.

Nathan stared at her, nostrils flaring, eyes flashing fire. 'As you knew it wasn't true, I don't see how it could have hurt you at all!'

'Oh, don't you?' Rachel flung back in outrage, pushed way beyond caution. 'Well, let me tell you something, Nathan Wade. It hurt like hell. It hurt me as it would hurt any woman who loved a man!'

The confession staggered her as much as it clearly shook him. Rachel closed her eyes in despair. She hadn't meant to say it, to give away so much. But now that she had revealed how she felt she could not take it back. Not even to defend herself. Steeling herself, she looked at him defiantly.

Nathan dragged a hand through his hair, a clear sign of agitation. 'Are you trying to tell me you love me?' he challenged, and his tone was far less aggressive than before.

'Yes. I love you,' she confirmed steadily, and, letting out a shaken breath, Nathan dragged a hand through his hair again, leaving it tousled.

'And how many of the chinless wonders you date have you said that to?' he asked curtly, making her flinch, though she hadn't expected him to believe her.

'None,' she responded honestly, for that was the only weapon she had left. 'For the simple reason you're the only man I've ever fallen in love with.'

He laughed mockingly. 'Am I supposed to be honoured?' he taunted, and that cut her to the quick, for she was baring her soul to him and all he could do was cut it to ribbons.

She knew she had paled, and she had to swallow once, twice, before her throat would work properly. 'If you loved me, I guess you would be honoured. So that answers one question, doesn't it? You don't love me,' she said huskily.

He stared at her, jaw flexing with tension. 'Did I ever give you the impression that I did?' he asked tautly, and she shook her head resignedly.

'No, you never did. In fact, I didn't even know

you wanted me until a couple of days ago. You're very good at hiding your feelings.'

Nathan opened his mouth to say something, then clearly thought better of it. He shook his head as if he needed to clear it, and his answer was strangely stilted. 'It's—er—something I've perfected over the years. It comes in handy in my line of work.'

'Yes, I imagine it does,' she said tiredly, worn out by the emotional outburst of the past few minutes. She had never felt so vulnerable in her life. 'God, this is such a mess. I didn't mean to embarrass you by telling you I loved you. It just slipped out.'

Nathan let out a long breath and flexed his shoulders, easing some of the tension in them. 'The truth often does, unless you're a cautious fellow like me. Your confession took me by surprise, but I wasn't embarrassed by it.'

Rachel found a weak smile from somewhere. 'Nevertheless, you'd rather I hadn't said it. I suppose you get protestations of love all the time from your women?' Lord, how she hated the very thought of them.

'Not that many,' he denied, eyeing her curiously. 'I tend to discourage it. I've never told any woman I loved her, either. I promised myself I would never say it until I meant it.'

She didn't really want to hear this, she thought, rubbing at her forehead, feeling the beginnings of a headache there. 'Well, if you need someone to confirm that claim, you can always send them to me!' she offered with a faint attempt at humour.

Though she didn't see it, Nathan's gaze softened, and he shook his head slowly. 'No, I don't think I will,' he said quietly, and colour stung her cheeks at the gentle snub.

'Fine. Do as you please. Oh, and you needn't worry that I will make a pest of myself. You'll never have to fear hearing those three little words from me again,' she told him shortly, coming very close to the end of her tether.

'Now that would be a shame,' he returned wryly, and, thinking she had surely misheard, Rachel blinked at him.

'What? What did you say?'

Nathan rubbed his thumb down the bridge of his nose and sighed. 'I said it would be a shame if you didn't say it to me again,' he repeated obligingly, and she stared at him incredulously.

'That's a ridiculous thing to say!' she exclaimed, hurt that he should make fun of her this way. She had thought better of him.

'Not from where I'm standing it isn't,' he countered, and her eyes took on the glitter of unshed tears.

'This isn't funny!'

He spread his hands soothingly. 'It isn't intended to be.'

It was all too much. She had been emotionally battered from all sides, and she didn't need this. 'I don't understand you!' she cried in exasperation. All she wanted to do was bury her head in her pillow and howl.

To her dismay, he had the gall to smile. 'I'm not so hard to understand if you remember what happened the other night,' he responded, and she gasped in shock.

'If you're referring to the fact that we made love, I fail to see the point!' she declared thickly. He was going too far.

Nathan tutted in mild reproof. 'Not that. I was referring to the fact that I lost at cards,' he said pointedly, but Rachel was too emotionally drained to make the connection.

'If you're trying to tell me something, Nathan, just do it. If not, I'd rather you left. I'll make my own way to Grandfather's later,' she told him wearily. She needed time to lick her wounds, and she didn't want him there whilst she did it. To her surprise and annoyance, Nathan shook his head.

'I don't think I'm going anywhere right now,' he refused, and she glared at him through over-bright eyes.

'I think you've had more than your pound of flesh. If you had any decency, you'd just go,' she insisted, turning away from him and walking to the window, where she gripped the sill until her knuckles whitened and stared out blankly at a view which usually charmed her.

'I guess I'm not that decent,' he countered mildly, and she swung round to face him.

'Nathan!' she began to protest, but he held up a hand.

'Rachel, has it never occurred to you that if I hid one thing from you I could hide another?' he asked her simply.

'What more is there?' He'd told her he didn't love her and that was all she needed to know. It was cruel of him to linger and prolong her agony this way.

'Just about everything, by the looks of it,' he observed sardonically, rubbing a hand around his jaw and eyeing her ruefully.

'I told you this isn't funny! I'm tired of your games!' she cried in exasperation, and he quickly closed the distance separating them, taking her by the shoulders, giving her a tiny shake.

'I'm not playing games now. Pay attention, for this is important. Answer me this. Did you mean it when you said you loved me?' he asked, holding her eyes, searching them.

Taunted beyond reason, she set her jaw mutinously. 'I thought I did. I'm not so sure now!' she snapped, and though she could scarcely credit it he smiled brightly.

'Rachel Shaw, you once told me that I would fall one day and fall hard. Sweetheart, can't you feel the ground shaking beneath your feet right now?' he asked gently, and her throat closed over as what he had been trying to tell her by various means began to sink in. Could he really be telling her he loved her too? Oh, how she wanted it to be true, but it was so incredible she didn't dare take it seriously for fear of getting hurt.

'That's just the underground. It passes right under here,' she retorted facetiously, whilst her heart waited anxiously for his answer.

He nodded soberly. 'OK, I deserve that. Why should you believe me when I've done nothing but lie to you?'

She stared up at him, scarcely daring to breathe. She would have asked him to pinch her to prove she wasn't dreaming, but dared not interrupt him now.

'What have you lied about?' Her brain was so addled she couldn't think of a thing.

He laughed, but it was against himself. 'I lied when I said I would never fall in love. The truth is I fell in love a long time ago.'

Her lips parted on a tiny gasp. 'You did?' she asked on a trembling sigh.

'Oh, yes,' Nathan confirmed with a nod. 'The trouble was, I fell for a woman who I honestly believed to be bad news.'

Rachel closed her eyes briefly, feeling a bubble of joy beginning to expand within her. He *was* saying he loved her, for who else fitted the description? Suddenly all her tiredness vanished like morning mist. Mastering her excitement, she looked up at him nonchalantly. 'You're beginning to interest me. Tell me more.'

Nathan laughed softly, though his eyes were deadly serious. 'I was determined that she would never know how I felt. I knew if she knew I would be lost.'

Her heart tripped, and it was hard to keep playing it cool. 'I think I know this story. So you kept her at a distance with words,' she supplied, and he first looked surprised, then rueful.

'You worked that out, did you?'

Rachel finally allowed a soft smile to curve her lips. 'Eventually. Then what happened?' she encouraged huskily, the pulse in her throat rushing along at an amazing pace.

One eyebrow rose in a way she found more endearing the more often she saw it. 'You're determined to hear a full confession?'

'Nothing else will do,' she told him honestly, for it would not. So much had been said, she needed to hear the truth from his own lips.

'This part doesn't reflect on me very well. You see, I discovered I could have her without committing myself. I was selfish enough to take advantage of her terms. At the time it seemed ideal, but...' Here he pulled a wry face, and Rachel frowned.

'But what?'

Absently his hands began to smooth up and down her silk-covered arms in a soothing caress. 'I began to get the feeling something wasn't quite right about her. Sometimes she didn't seem to be who I thought she was.'

Rachel couldn't resist mocking him. 'But I thought you were so sure about her?'

With a deep sigh Nathan pulled her unresisting body close and wrapped his arms around her. 'So did I. Now, of course, I realise what it was. You weren't that woman and never had been. I'd been protecting myself from someone who simply didn't exist. My only excuse for continuing to believe the ''lie'' was that I had never been in love before. It made me feel uncomfortably vulnerable. I didn't like it.'

Rachel buried her face in his neck, her own arms sliding around his waist. It felt so good to be there, and she knew now that she could stay. 'I know that feeling. I didn't like it either. I'd always been wary of love, because of my parents, and when I fell for you and you were so distant... The only way I could protect myself was to make sure you never knew I loved you.'

'Exactly,' Nathan agreed, rubbing his cheek against the silky softness of her hair. 'I hid my feelings because I couldn't run the risk of letting the woman I thought you were have that kind of power over me.'

'She wasn't very nice, was she?' Rachel teased softly.

'She was horrendous. When I discovered I'd fallen for her...'

She laughed huskily. 'It must have given you a nasty jolt.'

'That's putting it mildly.' Nathan grimaced, pressing a gentle kiss to the tender skin of her neck, making her shiver in pleasure. 'I'm sorry I fought so hard and dirty, but I was desperate.'

Rachel sighed, her hands running over his back in lazy circles. 'I'm sorry for what I did, too. Playing a trick on you seemed like a good idea, but I soon realised I'd dug myself into a hole I couldn't get out of,' she confided huskily, and heard the soft rumble of laughter in his chest.

'You certainly had me on a piece of string.'

She raised her head to look up at him. 'Have you stopped being angry with me?'

Nathan smiled wryly. 'You kind of ended it abruptly when you told me you loved me.'

'And you're no longer afraid of the power I have over you?'

Blue eyes scorched her with the strength of his feelings. 'I'm yours to command,' he declared throatily.

'In that case I think you should finish the story, don't you?'

'Is there something I've forgotten to tell you?' he queried innocently, but there was nothing innocent about the gleam in his eye.

Her green eyes took on a gleam of their own. 'You'd better tell me, Nathan, or you'll be sorry!' she warned him, and his husky laugh sent shivers down her spine.

Cupping her head in his palms, he looked down into her eyes. 'I love you, Rachel Shaw. I've loved you in silence for too long. God willing, I'll tell you I love you every day for the next sixty years,' he declared thickly, and her lips parted on a slow, sultry smile.

'That's all I wanted to hear,' she sighed, reaching up to meet his descending lips halfway. 'I love you too, Nathan,' she breathed, just before his lips settled on hers and the world faded away.

MILLS & BOON®
Makes any time special™

Mills & Boon publish 29 new titles every month. Select from...

Modern Romance™   Tender Romance™

Sensual Romance™

Medical Romance™ Historical Romance™

MAT2

FREE!

4 Books

and a surprise gift!

We would like to take this opportunity to thank you for reading this Mills & Boon® book by offering you the chance to take FOUR more specially selected titles from the Modern Romance™ series absolutely FREE! We're also making this offer to introduce you to the benefits of the Reader Service™ —

- ★ FREE home delivery
- ★ FREE gifts and competitions
- ★ FREE monthly Newsletter
- ★ Books available before they're in the shops
- ★ Exclusive Reader Service discounts

Accepting these FREE books and gift places you under no obligation to buy; you may cancel at any time, even after receiving your free shipment. Simply complete your details below and return the entire page to the address below. *You don't even need a stamp!*

YES! Please send me 4 free Modern Romance books and a surprise gift. I understand that unless you hear from me, I will receive 6 superb new titles every month for just £2.40 each, postage and packing free. I am under no obligation to purchase any books and may cancel my subscription at any time. The free books and gift will be mine to keep in any case.

P0ZEB

Ms/Mrs/Miss/Mr ....Initials..
BLOCK CAPITALS PLEASE

Surname...

Address...

....

....Postcode ....

Send this whole page to:
UK: The Reader Service, FREEPOST CN8I, Croydon, CR9 3WZ
EIRE: The Reader Service, PO Box 4546, Kilcock, County Kildare (stamp required)